Five Dares

ELI EASTON

RIPTIDE
PUBLISHING

To my own true bff.

TABLE OF Contents

Dare
#1

Chapter ONE

May 2017
Jake

"...two ... three ... four ..." Andy's count was infuriatingly slow. The lit firecrackers we held sparked and sizzled. A mix of exhilaration and dread made goose bumps break out all over my body.

We stood next to a swimming pool at a private party in Brooklyn. It was the night of our college graduation, and maybe that made everyone crazier than usual. Andy was definitely in peak crazy zone tonight. He and I stood facing one other, a brown-wrapped firecracker the size and shape of a hotdog lying across each of our four palms. The base of my spine tingåled and my heart pumped *ba-bum ba-bum ba-bum*, like the strokes on a drum on a slave ship in some old movie.

God, I never felt more alive than when Andy and I were performing a stunt!

This particular trick had started with Andy showing up by the pool, holding aloft four candle bombs. "Where's my man Jake?" he'd called out.

I'd been in position near the pool, pretending to listen to a group conversation. At Andy's prompt, I stepped forward. "What are you doing, bro?"

He brandished the firecrackers. "You and me, Jakey. We light these puppies and hold on to them for the count of ten. You in?"

The crowd reaction washed over us in an electric rush. There were hoots of encouragement from the guys, and some girls lost their shit, especially Andy's girlfriend, Amber. God, it was great. Andy was a show-off, and I was always willing to get swept along in his wild wake. His eyes stayed locked on me, but I knew he was soaking in every mote of the attention as everyone at the party gathered around the pool to see what would happen.

Andy drew attention naturally. He was so damn good-looking and charismatic with his bleached-blond hair, huge blue eyes, and wide smile. When he wasn't being all serious, when he was playful and wild and free and reckless like he was tonight, no one could resist him.

Certainly not me. Never me. Though I pretended otherwise.

"It's too dangerous," I said with a *pfft* of dismissal. "You've lost your mind."

"Only the good die young, man. Come on."

"No way." I shook my head, my voice firm. "We'll blow our hands off. You're crazy."

"I dare ya, Jake Masterson. I. Dare. You." He continued to hold out the firecrackers.

"Stop it!" Amber insisted. "Andy, *please.*"

There were hoots in the crowd. More people came out of the house to watch.

With a dramatic roll of my eyes, and a loud grumble about death wishes and how dangerous it was, I slowly reached out and took two of the firecrackers, acting all reluctant. Andy loved to fuck with people's heads, and he said I was the best wingman ever. I certainly did my best to help freak people out.

He held up the two brown-wrapped candle bombs he still had left. "Right, then! Ladies and gentlemen, boys and girls, or *however* you define your innies and outties, I give you . . . the last great dare of NYU class of 2017!"

There were smatterings of applause and more rumbles of worry and fear. Yeah. We had them hooked.

"We'll need four volunteers with lighters or matches." I held out my open hands, rolling each firecracker so it was positioned partially off the side of my palm, wick facing out.

He did the same as four guys came up, lighters in hand. Andy eyed my palms to make sure I'd positioned the firecrackers just so.

"Drop them, you guys! I swear to God!" That was Amber. Her voice sounded both tearful and angry. "This isn't funny!"

"No shit. Dudes! You're going to get yourselves killed!" some random guy called out.

But Andy's blue eyes had danced with life, brighter than the lit fuses, the way they only did when he was putting himself, and usually me too, in imminent danger, when he was willfully breaking every damn rule. His eyes had stayed locked on mine while a naughty grin beamed on his face. That grin said: *You and me, Jakey. You and me.*

"... seven ... eight ..."

I inched my hands higher, prepared to toss the firecrackers into the pool the second he got to—

"... nine ..."

That's when the world exploded.

ANDY

I could blame that infamous firecracker dare on the two beers I'd had at the party, but that would be a lie. The truth was, I'd been itching for trouble before we'd even arrived.

I had to pick up Amber, so Jake took the train with a few other students to the party. The graduation bash was being hosted by some guy whose parents were out of town. It sounded like a nice change from the usual frat parties, a chance to get off campus, and there was supposed to be a pool. So everyone we knew said they were going. When I got to the house, I started walking around with Amber holding on to a back loop of my jeans. I was looking for a) beer and b) Jake.

I found the beer keg first. I poured a glass for Amber and me, and drank mine fast. Refilled my glass. Amber started to talk to some girl she knew, and I went looking for Jake. I finally spotted him talking to a brunette off in a corner of the living room. She was his type— bookish but cute, petite, part Asian, and wearing librarian glasses.

She laughed at something he said, totally focused on him. And why wouldn't she be? Jake had clearly made an effort for the party. He had on a purple, long-sleeve, button-down shirt that made his pale skin and dark hair look paler and darker than usual. The shirt was fitted, and his jeans too. He wasn't a huge guy, but he had a great face and big brown eyes. He looked good. He also seemed to like the girl he was chatting up. Only someone who knew him well, the way I did, would see he was nervous talking to her. His throat had light-pink blotches, and he licked his lips more often than usual.

Watching them, I felt a rush of jealousy. For a moment, I couldn't breathe. It was ridiculous, and I knew it. It wasn't that I was jealous about the *girl*. Whatever. No, but this was our last night out together before Jake left for California. The "terrible two-o," as Jake jokingly called us, was breaking up. He'd landed a real job with a software company and I, I was headed to Harvard Law. Jake insisted we'd still be in touch and all that, but it wouldn't be the same. Jake was going off to his adult life, and I'd be on the other side of the country. For tonight, at least, I wanted to spend time with my best friend. I wanted Jake's attention *on me*.

Instead of interrupting him, I headed outside to poke around, get the lay of the land. That reckless itch was building inside me, pushing me to act. I needed something, something dangerous, something exciting. I just didn't know what it was going to be. I contemplated the pool for a moment, but there were too many people already in it, and I couldn't come up with any brilliant stunt to do in a pool.

The garage door was open and the lights were on. There was an extra keg in there, waiting to be summoned. I looked around on the shelves, bypassing tools and cans of oil, various balls and sporting gear. That's when I found the box of firecrackers.

"It'll be awesome!" I put my hand on Jake's arm. I kept my voice low and looked around to make sure we were alone in the garage. "I just tested one. I counted to fifteen before it went off. I'll make the dare for ten and we'll have five seconds to spare. We'll stand by the pool and toss them in the minute I reach the count."

Jake crossed his arms and looked at me with that mix of *I-want-to-but-I-don't* on his face. "What if it goes off early? We could get seriously fucked up."

"Won't happen. And even if it does, we'll be fine. Watch." I placed the firecracker across my open palm so that the wick and a good inch of the cardboard tube was hanging off the side.

"And?"

"A firecracker is an explosion. When it goes off, it's going to expand and it'll use the path of least resistance. With our hands open, all the energy would go up into the air. Whoosh." I mimicked the explosion with the outspread fingers of my other hand. "Our palms would barely be scratched. Now *this*—" I closed my fist around the firecracker and gripped it tight in a fist. "*This* would be stupid. The energy of the explosion would have nowhere to go, so it'd rip up skin and bones, but like this . . ." I went back to the open palm. "It's harmless. Trust me. But, fuck, it'll look dangerous, won't it? People will lose their shit." I grinned at him.

I could tell I'd hooked Jake. He might deny it, but he got off on our stunts as much as I did. He pursed his lips as if trying not to smile, then he did anyway, unable to contain it. "You're the best bullshitter I ever met. Like, if bullshitting were an Olympic sport, you'd be Michael Phelps. You know that, right?"

I felt a glow of pleasure at his words. "It's called showmanship, my friend. So wanna do it? This is the last time. Our last dare. We'll go out legends."

He snorted. "Hopefully the 'going out' part will be figurative and not literal."

Yeah, he was totally caving. I gave him puppy-dog eyes to seal the deal. I was manipulating him a little, but Jake knew me well enough to be on to me. And the sucky thing was, it actually *was* the last time. The last time for the Andy and Jake Show, for the "two guys who'll do anything." I knew it, and I hated it. Despite my excitement over the stunt, a nasty pang twisted in my gut.

"One last dare, *Jake*. You up for it?" I pushed, more to assuage the pang than because I really doubted he'd agree. I held out my fist.

He nodded slowly and bumped my hand. "Let's do this, then. The last show."

"The last show," I agreed.

In the end, it turned out the information I'd quickly read on a blog about firework explosions wasn't *entirely* accurate.

Chapter
TWO

JAKE

That night at the hospital was a living hell. The nurses woke me up *constantly*. I'd hit my head pretty good on the concrete lip of the pool after the firecrackers exploded, and I had the goose egg to prove it. They kept waking me every few hours on concussion watch. I wanted to sob, *Just let me fucking sleep.*

Besides the irritating pupil-check brigade, my hands hurt like a son of a bitch. They were both wrapped wrist to fingertip in bulky bandages like a prize fighter. It was kind of a cool look—Andy would probably like it. If not for, you know, the burns. It felt like the bandages were lined with ground glass or maybe razor blades. Even twitching a finger caused a sensation like my skin was being ripped off. And, of course, twitching was exactly what I did every time the nurses asked me about the pain.

I was on some good drugs, and if I could keep my hands perfectly motionless, the pain faded away. But they were *hands*. I would unconsciously go to move them—to pull up the sheet, scratch my nose, or reach for the glass by my bed—and I'd be in agony again. The actual pain level had to be bad if it hurt that much despite the drugs. On top of that, the reality of what had happened was slowly sinking in.

This wasn't like any of the other stunts Andy and I had pulled over the years. I'd never gotten hurt before, at least not seriously. In fact, I'd gotten way more cuts and bruises playing one-on-one basketball or touch football with Andy than I had on our dares. But this . . . this was going to be a serious problem. I didn't know how serious until I talked to the doctor. The nurses promised me he'd be by first thing in the morning.

Dr. Benji came in just before 8 a.m. He looked like he was playing dress-up in his lab coat. It had a jaunty belt at the waist and was a blinding shade of pure white that was matched only by the brilliance of his teeth. He was Asian, had straight black hair past his shoulders, probably weighted ninety pounds soaking wet, and appeared to be about my age. Seriously. If I'd been a bar bouncer, there was no way I'd be fooled by his fake ID. As a physician, he wasn't exactly confidence inspiring.

"Hey there! I'm Dr. Benji!" He grinned. Then he pouted his lips. "You boys are lucky to not have lost some fingers." He waggled his own fingers at me.

"It wasn't supposed to actually be dangerous," I muttered.

Dr. Benji stared at me, a little frown between his eyes. "Holding on to a lit firecracker is not dangerous? How do you figure that, buddy?"

"Uh, well, they were in our open palms." I went to demonstrate by moving my hands and winced at the pain, giving up instantly. I gritted my teeth as the sharp daggers subsided. "The . . . the explosion was supposed to go *upward* and . . ."

I trailed off, seeing the wide-eyed disbelief on Dr. Benji's face. He was studying me like I was a total and complete idiot. He had a point.

"Never mind," I said.

He glanced at my chart, flipped a page. "Okay! So. Second- and third-degree burns on pretty much the underside of your entire hand. Both hands. Um-hmm. Um-hmm." He looked up, his eyes bright and cheerful. "Yup. Pretty bad. Hope you don't have any exciting plans for the summer, Mr. Masterson."

I regarded my two mummy-wrapped hands, feeling the first wafts of panic. "But . . . how long do I need to wear these?"

"Six to eight weeks, buster. You need to use your hands as little as possible. The less you use, the quicker you heal. Got it? So I hope you have a patient girlfriend." He tittered.

My mind immediately went into the gutter.

It must have shown on my face, because Dr. Benji's mouth dropped open and his cheeks pinkened. "For feeding you! And helping you dress. Things like, um, that." His eyes went wide with embarrassment and he stared back down at my chart. "Okay! So, you are very lucky. You narrowly escaped the need for skin grafting. Or, you know, losing your entire hand at the wrist. But still. The damage is serious. The top layers of your skin were fried. Kind of like sausages on a grill."

"Great."

"So it will take a while for what itsy bitsy layer of healthy skin you have left to heal and grow new layers. You know? And for the damaged layers to peel off." He was back to his cheerful tone. "So. No using your hands, right? You damage that last bit of good skin, you may yet end up with surgery and skin grafts. Let's avoid that, whaddya say?" He winked.

Now it was my turn to stare. "When you say 'no using your hands,' do you mean I won't be able to type?"

Dr. Benji laughed with genuine amusement. "Heavens no! Definitely no typing. That's the last thing you should do. That would pull all kinds of skin and tendons." He mocked typing in the air with delicate fingers. "Plus, it would hurt like a bear. No, you want to keep your hands as immobile as possible until your new skin is completely healed."

"Oh shit." I wanted to cover my face with my hands, but just starting to bring them up reminded me of the inadvisability of that idea. And that made me realize how hard this was going to be. Every other minute I was going to start to do something only to realize I couldn't do it. And that was just ordinary day-to-day stuff. That didn't even touch on my job, which I was supposed to be starting in two weeks.

For a moment I imagined myself showing up for work with my hands bandaged like this. *Hey, here I am, reporting for duty! One small thing, though—I can't type, hope that's okay. Or hold a pen. Or open my desk drawers. Or even, you know, get inside the damn building, because I can't grasp the door handle. Other than that, I'm raring to go!*

I closed my eyes and groaned. Dread and a sense of shame at having been very, very foolish prickled my neck and tightened my belly. I was so, so screwed. I was so getting Andy back for this.

Only the moment I thought it, I realized something that hadn't occurred to me: Andy had been holding firecrackers too.

My eyes flew open. "Shit. My friend Andy. Is he okay? He didn't lose any fingers, did he?" I couldn't even imagine that. Andy was so physical. The entire world was like one huge game to him. If he didn't have a ball of some sort in his hands, it was a stick or a dart or a bat. He had beautiful hands, crazy dexterous. Not that I thought a lot about my best friend's hands.

Okay, I did. I thought a lot about my best friend's hands.

Dr. Benji relieved my fears. "He's in the same boat you are, pretty much." He winked at me again. "Which means the two of you will need someone else to paddle." He laughed, *ho ho ho*, at his own joke.

This guy was a real comedian.

"So he didn't require skin grafts either?"

"Not so far. And he won't if he's careful and follows doctor's orders, just like you." He gave me a warning glare that was as harmless as the bark of a Chihuahua. "Look at the bright side, though! Turns out you don't have a concussion and you won't have much scarring in the end. Cool, right?" He raised his hand up for a high five, and then, as if remembering I wasn't supposed to move my hand, grimaced and dropped it again. "So, uh, yeah. See ya, sport. Okay? Hey, watch out for the lime Jell-O!"

He walked out, laughing. Jesus Christ. Fucking modern healthcare.

I lay in the hospital bed trying to figure out what the hell I was going to do now. I needed to call my sister, Sierra, and confess how royally I'd screwed up. She was two years older than me, and had helped me get a job as a programmer at the company where she worked, Neverware. And then what? I was supposed to move to California on Saturday. Could I even travel like this? No way could I move boxes or drive my car. Hell, I couldn't even get my dick out of my pants to take a piss.

Holy crap. How was I going to *eat*?

It struck me that I was helpless as a baby. And that was for at least six weeks, maybe as long as eight. What was the point of going to California if I couldn't work? A programmer needed to type. That was pretty much a minimum skill set right there. I couldn't stay on campus, our place was already rented out to someone else. And wherever I landed, I'd need someone to take care of me.

My summer was ruined. And maybe more than that too.

On the bright side, I could ask the nurse to bring me a couple of servings of that lime Jell-O. Maybe I'd get lucky and that shit would kill me.

ANDY

The first thing I saw when I woke up in the hospital was my dad. He was sitting in a chair drawn up close to my bed, watching me with a blank face.

I closed my eyes again, inwardly groaning. Oh God, what had I done to deserve this hell? My hands were both bandaged and hurting. Worse, Jake was hurt too. I wasn't even sure how badly he'd been hurt, because we'd been driven to the hospital in separate cars. The nurse in the ER told me he hadn't lost any digits and was "doing as well as could be expected," but I was still worried. Now on top of all that I had to deal with my father. Talk about a seriously crappy day.

"I know you're awake, Andrew. So you might as well stop pretending."

I opened my eyes. Looking at my dad was like looking into a mirror that aged me twenty-five years. His face had a few lines and his blond hair was gray at the temples, but mostly he seemed old because of the serious set of his . . . everything. He wore glasses and dress pants, a shirt, and a tie, even now. What was it, like, 8 a.m.? He and my mom had been at my graduation the day before, but drove home after the ceremony. It was a four-hour drive from our house near Boston to NYU, so, yeah, he couldn't have been happy to have to turn around and drive right back. I could add exhaustion to the list of his reasons to be pissed at me. Wonderful.

"What on earth were you thinking?" he asked.

I swallowed, but my throat felt like I'd been snacking on a bucket of sand. "Coffee?" I croaked.

"Coffee," he muttered with a huff, as though I'd asked for a hit of meth. He grabbed a glass with a sippy straw from the nightstand and held it up for me. I struggled upright a little on my elbows and drank. It was warm water that tasted vaguely of chemicals. It was disgusting, but at least it soothed my throat.

"Well, Andrew," my dad began as he put the glass back, "you've ruined your summer, if not your entire future. I hope you're pleased with yourself."

I bit back a sarcastic reply. There was no escaping this ordeal of a conversation, so I had to grit my teeth and bear it. And, to be honest, I deserved it. I *had* miscalculated. Hugely. I should never have rushed a stunt like that. I should have tested those firecrackers way more thoroughly. *Damn it.* I'd hurt myself, but more importantly, I'd hurt Jake. And that was unacceptable. This convo with my dad was just the cherry on top of the shit pile.

"My future is not going to be ruined if I don't get to work at Kosen & Kosen this summer," I said calmly, trying to keep the conversation from escalating.

"It was on your five-year plan," Dad pointed out.

"I know that. But I'm just starting Harvard Law in the fall. It's not like I won't have other opportunities for internships."

He frowned. "Letting down a prestigious agency at the last minute is the perfect way to ruin your reputation before you even get started. And there'll be a suspicious gap on your résumé."

God, my résumé. The holy fucking grail. It wasn't as if other twenty-two-year-old future lawyers didn't have a single summer in their lives when they didn't work. I was sure there had to be others who were backpacking in Europe, or sailing around the Bahamas—or lying around recovering from burns.

"I'm injured, Dad." I sounded more irritated than I should have. "I have a good excuse for bailing on my internship. And it's not like I was going to be that valuable at Kosen & Kosen anyway. It was just a clerk job."

My mom had gotten me that internship—not at her law firm, that would be too nepotistic, but at a firm she worked with frequently. I'd gotten the impression it was more a favor to her than a critical need for my help on their part.

My dad's frown didn't shift one iota. "Obviously, you'll have to say you were injured, but we need to come up with a story about how it happened. You certainly can't tell them you were doing something idiotic on a dare. No one wants a lawyer who has no ability to foresee the most obvious consequences."

I gritted my teeth harder.

My dad's voice softened, became more worried than angry. "What were you thinking, Andrew? I'd really like to understand. The nurse said you were both *holding* lit firecrackers? Were you drunk? High? Was it Jake's idea? I thought you were finally done with all that nonsense."

There was so much wrong with that statement. A spark of anger flared in my chest. I hated it when my dad talked smack about Jake. And yes, I did sometimes get drunk. But I was way more responsible than most guys my age. My dad didn't have to act like I was a loser. Not when I'd busted my ass doing what he wanted for so many years. Hell, I'd just graduated at the top of my class at NYU.

"It was my idea, not Jake's," I said in a low, tight voice. "It was a stunt that went wrong, that's all. Yes, it was stupid, but I can't change it now."

"A stunt! You and your interest in David Blaine and all that magic nonsense. It's enough of a waste of time that you watch it on video or read about it. But to try to *do* it? Don't you realize these things are dangerous? What is the point?"

I was surprised he even knew I was into David Blaine. So he actually paid attention to the shows I watched or books I read? The thought was worrying.

"Sometimes there isn't 'a point,'" I said calmly. "Sometimes you do things because they're funny. Or exciting. Or they seem like a good idea at the time. I already admitted the firecracker idea was dumb. It was a mistake, and I should have been better than that. What else do you want me to say?" I started to clench my fists, as I often did when talking to my dad. Agony shot through both hands, making me writhe on the bed.

Fucking hell. Don't move your hands. Idiot.

"Should I ring for the nurse?" my dad asked worriedly. He reached out and brushed the hair out of my eyes. Crap. Just when I wanted to shut him out, he had to be nice.

20268461

"No, I'm fine." I gasped through the pain. I already felt loopy from the drugs they'd given me overnight. I just needed to . . . not move. I lay there, staring at the ceiling and panting.

"Mom?" I asked to change the subject.

"She was going to come back with me, but I told her not to. The doctor who called us said it wasn't critical, and your mother had a full slate of meetings this morning. But she sends her love. I need to text her and let her know how you're doing."

"Okay." I let my breath out slowly as the pain began to fade—thank fuck.

"Well," my dad said grudgingly. "From what I understand there'll be no permanent damage. I hate to say it, but maybe this injury will turn out to be a good thing. Maybe this is what you needed to finally wise up and stop with this daredevil business. It's time to grow up, Andrew. Your entire future is on the line now."

He was right. My future was on the line. But then, when had it ever not been? It seemed like it had been absolutely critical that I do everything right since I started earning a report card in first grade.

As the pain left my hands, I relaxed on the bed, feeling miserable. All I'd wanted was . . . what? To do one more spectacular dare with my best friend? To somehow hold on to Jake?

To somehow hold on to Jake.

The nurse had given me the impression Jake's injuries were much like mine. So maybe he wouldn't be leaving for California. The thought made me feel considerably less miserable.

"The doctor says you can't do much of anything all summer. I suppose we'll have to hire you a nurse. Your mother and I can't just take off work to wait on you day and night."

"No. I know that. Will the insurance cover a nurse?"

"Of course it will! Physical therapy too. Unlike *most* people's insurance. Good insurance can save you millions, you know." My dad sounded pleased with himself. He took insurance seriously. He was a financial planner, and believe me, it wasn't just a day job for him. Sometimes I wondered if he'd ever thought about anything else in his life.

He rambled on about the importance of health insurance for a while. "We could afford a much better hospital, but they're going to release you tomorrow morning anyway, so there's no point in having you transferred."

"No," I said quickly. "I'm fine here." I'd rather be where Jake was than in the most luxurious hotel in the world. "So, Dad . . . about this summer."

Chapter
THREE

Andy

My dad finally left, and all I wanted to do was see Jake. The hospital we'd been sent to was in a huge old building in Brooklyn. My father turned up his nose at the place, but it honestly wasn't that bad. My private room on the second floor was decent except that Jake wasn't in it. I had to charm the nurses ruthlessly before one told me that Jake was up on the tenth floor. She wouldn't agree to take me up there, though. Said she was too busy and "maybe later."

Right. Like I was going to wait. I'd try texting or calling him, but with my bandaged mitts, I couldn't use my phone. And, anyway, I had to see for myself, in person, that he was okay. I got the nurse to put the IV on a rolling stand for me so I could go to the bathroom and sit up in the chair. After that, it was easy enough to sneak out of my room. I managed to operate the elevator buttons with my elbow. And there I was wandering around the hospital with a rolling IV stand I was steering with my forearm, my two hands taped up like Muhammad Ali, wearing nothing but a hospital gown, socks with that nonslip stuff on the bottom, and, thankfully, my underwear. Well, I'd done stupider things, that was for sure.

Unfortunately, the pain meds were stronger than I'd accounted for. Loopty-loop, man. It was fun to feel semi-stoned, but not helpful. I finally found room 1023. The door of the room was open, and I peeked in. It was a small room, dingy, with two beds. One bed was mostly hidden by a drawn curtain. Jake was in the bed closest to the door, and he was awake. The head of his bed was raised so he was almost in a sitting position. His cell phone was on his lap on top of the sheets, bracketed by his two bandaged hands. They looked an awful lot like mine. They lay limp on his thighs as he stared down at his phone morosely. There might even have been a hint of moisture in his eyes. He looked miserable, and my heart did a sick little throb. *Oh Jake. Bro.* Guilt gnawed at me.

"Hey," I said, walking all the way into the room. I didn't have any trouble mustering a contrite expression. Hell, even my stomach was contrite. It was doing its damnedest to hide behind my spine.

Jake glanced up at me sharply. When he saw it was me, he frowned, making me feel even worse. I knew Jake's expressions like I knew the back of my hand—or *had* known the back of my hand; it might be scarred after this. Jake should look ready to punch me, but instead he appeared worried. About me. That was the kind of friend Jake was.

"Are you okay?" he asked.

I shrugged, taking care not to move my hands where they hung at my side. "Doctor says I'll heal, but I'm gonna be fucked up for a while. You? You have to have surgery or anything like that? Anything permanent? The nurses wouldn't give me the details." *The cruel bastards.*

He grimaced and looked down at his bandages. "All fingers accounted for and no surgery. At least, not unless I get infected or try to move around too much before it heals."

That was basically what the doctor had told me too. Jake's words should have been reassuring, but they weren't. Even the thought that Jake *could* have been hurt that badly, that one of my stunts could have disfigured him for life, freaked me the fuck out. I felt woozy and had to sit down. There was a visitor chair against the wall. I hooked my foot around one leg and dragged it closer to his bed, then collapsed into the thing, taking care not to upset my wheeling IV rack.

"Wow. Andy. I've never seen you turn the color of cottage cheese before. You gonna faint?"

I shook my head, but I was in no state to joke about it. Dots of black swam in my vision, and somehow I'd disturbed my hands despite not using them. They hurt like a bitch. "It's the drugs," I managed, closing my eyes.

I sank back in the chair, waiting for the dizziness and pain to pass. I felt a little better just being in the same room as Jake. He wasn't dead, and he didn't hate me. Or, at least, he was still talking to me. Maybe the hate would come later. I wouldn't blame him.

When I opened my eyes, though, Jake was looking at the wall, his face miserable again.

"You okay?" I asked. Stupid question.

He sniffed and shrugged, then laughed bitterly. "Fuck. I can't even rub my nose."

"I know."

He sighed. "The nurse helped me call Sierra just now. She's gonna talk to HR at Neverware for me. Hopefully they'll delay my start date. And not, you know, fire me before I even start working there."

"God, Jake. I'm so sorry."

He said nothing, just stared at the wall. Now I knew why he looked so miserable. And my own sense of guilt multiplied like extras in a zombie movie. I swallowed. "What did Sierra say exactly?"

He gave me a dark look. "That I'm a fucking idiot. Which, you know, fair point."

"She always did have a knack for stating the obvious," I teased. He didn't smile.

He worried his lip and stared at the wall some more, like maybe he was trying to conjure up a portal to a happier, simpler world. He was totally in Serious Jake mode.

Jake was the funniest guy I knew, but scratch that witty facade and you'd find a bone-deep worrier. He'd always taken things seriously, even back when we'd met in seventh grade. In high school he'd studied for tests and never ditched school. I'd done those things too—because if I hadn't, I'd have had to deal with my old man. But school was easy for me, and I'd always managed to do the bare minimum to make the dean's list and keep my folks happy. Jake's focus had intensified once we got to college. We'd roomed together for four years at NYU, so I could attest to his grueling study habits. Dear God, the Saturday nights when I'd had to drag Jake out of the room by the scruff of his neck.

Shortly after Jake and I met, Jake's dad left them. He'd been having an affair with some lady in his office, and she got pregnant, so he decided to divorce Jake's mom and move in with this other woman, marry her, and raise the kid. Basically leaving family number one to start family number two.

I still remembered the night Jake's mom dropped him off late at our place because shit was hitting the fan at their house. Lying in my bed in the dark, Jake choked out his biggest fear. Without his dad, he was the head of the family now. He would have to work—get a job that made good money so he could support himself and, if needed, take care of his mom and sister. No one would be there to be his safety net, to pay for things like college, to cover his bills if he couldn't find work. He was completely alone.

I'd tried to tell him it wouldn't be that way, that his dad would still be around, and his mom too. But Jake had utter conviction that he was completely responsible for himself, if not immediately, then right after high school. His parents didn't have a whole lot of money anyway—not like my family did. Their house was modest. His mom was a dental assistant and his dad an accountant for some tiny tax place in the mall. I'd always had everything I needed or wanted, and I figured I always would. So anything I could say to Jake sounded like platitudes. And we didn't really talk about that kind of thing much anyway—emotions. Emotions sucked, and we mostly pretended we didn't have them.

Jake worried, that was all. He'd studied hard to get honors in computer science so he could get a good job immediately. I knew how much the Neverware job meant to him.

I tried to reassure him. "They really liked you at the interview, you said. Plus Sierra works there. They won't drop you because you got hurt. That would be totally shitty. It's only a two-month delay."

"Yeah," Jake agreed with a sigh. "Sierra thought they'd probably just have me start the first of September since a bunch of people in the department are on vacation in August anyway. I hope they're cool with that. She says as long as I'm there in time for her wedding on September twenty-third, she won't kill me."

I swallowed a lump. "I really am sorry, Jake." I wished I could take it all back, that last stupid dare at the party. But life didn't work that way.

He looked at me. He must have been able to see how bad I felt, because his face softened. "Hey, I didn't have to agree to it. I thought it would work too."

"I thought it made sense."

"It totally made sense. Maybe the firecrackers were defective."

I bit my lip, feeling sheepish. "I noticed Spanish on the fireworks box. If they were from Mexico, they might have had stronger powder than American fireworks. Hell, they were probably illegal."

Jake blinked at me. "A fine time to bring that up, Sherlock."

I grimaced. "We did freak a lot of people out though?"

"Oh yeah. We were definitely memorable," Jake deadpanned with wide eyes. "We'll probably make YouTube's Darwin Awards."

We stared at each other. Despite how genuinely bad I felt for screwing up Jake's summer, and for both of us being injured, I couldn't help but see how ridiculous the whole situation was, how ridiculous *we* were. So when Jake's lips quirked up, my own laughter was right there. We started laughing and couldn't stop.

Jake held up his hands as if he wanted to cover his mouth, like he usually did when he laughed. But, of course, he couldn't, and *I* couldn't wipe my eyes, so we just sat there howling and holding out our mummy hands, and that made us both laugh harder.

"Oh God, that was the . . . the s-stupidest thing . . . we've ever done!" Jake choked out, barely understandable between gales of laughter.

"Nah. The quarry coulda been way worse," I managed.

Gradually our laughter died off. I could see it had cheered Jake up, but it didn't take long for his brown eyes to once again fill with worry. I had an urge to sit on his bed and give him a hug or at least pat his shoulder. Which was so not going to happen, even if I had my hands.

"What about your internship?" Jake asked, as if he'd just remembered it.

"Not happening." I shrugged.

"Sorry. That sucks for you too."

"Yeah. To tell you the truth, my dad's more upset about it than I am."

Jake snorted. "God, the spreadsheets that man's going to have to tweak."

I laughed. He knew my dad well. We both sat there for a while. My hands lay on my lap like dead fish.

"The next eight weeks are gonna be hell." Jake sighed. "My mom has to work. She can't be babysitting me twenty-four seven, even if I could stand living at home, which I can't. Sierra's in California, and you're as bad off as I am. There *is* no one else. You have Amber, but—"

"I don't have Amber. She broke up with me over text last night. Said if I wanted to kill myself, I could do it without her." I waggled my eyebrows at him.

His face struggled for a moment. And finally he managed to scrape up the fakest sympathetic expression ever. "I'm sorry?"

I laughed out loud. "Wow. You deserve an Emmy for that right there." I mimicked a simpering voice. "I'm . . . sorreee?" turning up the end comically.

He rolled his eyes but grinned. "Yeah. Not really sorry. I tried though. I get bro points for that. But I *am* sorry it was over a stunt. And I know your dad liked her."

"He did. But it's not like she was the love of my life."

Of course, that had never been the point of Amber. She was from Bostonian blue blood and her family had money. She was smart and attractive, but I really couldn't see a future with her, no matter how many boxes she ticked off on the ten-year plan. I always felt like I was on audition when I was with her, like she was judging me. And she only ever talked about spa appointments, traveling to fancy places like Cannes, and sailboats. Not that there was anything wrong with those things, but they weren't high on my list of priorities.

I'd rather hang with Jake. I cleared my throat. "Actually, I have some ideas about that. About the next eight weeks."

Jake looked at me with sudden interest. "Yeah? The Planinator is on it? Do your ideas involve me too?"

"Yes. Yes they do."

He looked both relieved and suspicious. Then again, Jake was always a little suspicious of my plans. I couldn't imagine why. "So tell me."

I kept my voice steady, my body relaxed in the chair. "We should go down to the cottage in Cape Cod, you and me. We're both going to need help, so we might as well be together. That way one person can help us both."

"Who's gonna help us there? No way am I letting your mom or dad anywhere near my naked body. I'd rather be put in a crate and hosed off for the next two months." He shuddered.

I made a horrified face. "God, no! They won't be there. They'll be in Boston working, as always. My insurance covers an in-home nurse, and I'm sure we can find one in the area. As for meals and all that, Emily can help us out."

"Emily?"

"The lady who cleans the cottage and stocks food and essentials when we're going down there. Her husband, Bob, does the outside maintenance. He can help too, if we need something done."

Jake regarded me warily. "What about showers and . . . like . . . the bathroom."

I shrugged. "If we wear loose pants with elastic and go commando, we don't need help with that. I managed to piss by myself this morning. Used the edge of the sink to get my pants down and leaned forward . . ." I demonstrated, standing up and leaning my upper body out over my legs, exaggerating it.

It made Jake laugh, like I knew it would. "Classy! Oh my God, now that would be a priceless video! What about wiping your ass? Or does the Planinator never need to take a dump?"

"We can probably rig something up. Jesus, give me a few hours to work out the kinks, Oh Impatient One. I've been disabled for less than half a day. I was thinking—they must have hooks and grabbers we can use, tools for people who have trouble using their hands. Maybe the hospital can set us up with stuff."

"Probably." Jake's eyes were still smoky, but the frown between his eyes had softened and he relaxed back onto the pillow. "There's all that accessibility stuff on Windows and iPhone. I've never used it, but it shouldn't be hard to set up. With voice command, we could at least surf the web and make phone calls. Watch porn." He smirked at me.

"Yeah, probably not the best idea." I held up my hands and raised my eyebrows.

His eyes widened as the implication sank in. "Oh, fuuuck. You *asshole*."

Then we were both laughing again. A pathetic, we-are-in-so-much-trouble sort of laugh.

When we finally wound down, Jake gave me a hairy eyeball. "I may not hate you for getting me into this mess right now, but by the end of the summer, I just might."

"Oh God, me too," I agreed, with a last, breathy chuckle.

"Cape Cod. Jesus. That was so not the way I was supposed to be spending my summer."

"We've had some great times at that cottage though. It won't totally suck."

My parents bought the waterfront cottage in Osterville on the Nantucket Sound when I was fifteen, and Jake and I had spent a lot of weeks there over the past six years.

"Yeah. If I didn't know better, I'd wonder if you did this on purpose to get me there with you for the summer."

His tone was joking, but I felt a rush of guilt all the same. Of course, I hadn't burned all four of our hands on purpose. But there *had* been something inside me lately, something that made me itch to push him. To push us. Our paths were forking away from each other at lightning speed. Our days at NYU were over, and there'd be no more coming in from classes to see Jake studying at his desk in our room, or walking across campus together to Patsy's Pizzeria in the winter, or lying in our respective beds shooting the shit for hours in the dark.

Had I sabotaged us unconsciously? Had some fucked-up part of me wanted to keep Jake close at any cost? Wow, that was so not cool.

"Hey, mopey, I'm kidding," he said quietly.

I blinked and focused on him.

"You look like you just ran over your puppy. You know I'm not blaming you, right?"

Jake. He was one hundred percent gold. "Well, it *was* my stupid idea. The least I can do is make sure your summer of healing doesn't entirely blow. If we're both forced to take the summer off, we should try to enjoy it as much as possible. Right? Consider it a mental health break."

Jake's eyes warmed considerably. "I guess so. At least I have a good excuse to be lazy." He held up his hands. "One thing though. If we do end up going to Cape Cod, there will *no dares*. All summer long. Swear?" He glowered at me sternly.

I gave him my best "who me?" expression. "What would we even have to dare about? Who can paddle the canoe fastest using their teeth?"

He chuckled, but his intense expression didn't waver. He knew my deflecting techniques all too well. "Swear to me, Andy."

"No dares," I promised sincerely.

Famous. Last. Words.

Dare #2

Chapter

FOUR

Andy

Jake's mom, Sandra, drove us to the cottage on Sunday. Jake, being Jake, felt guilty about it.

"I'm sorry you had to waste your one day off work," he told her when we were on the freeway. I was in the back seat chilling. It wasn't like I could do much to keep myself entertained with both hands wrapped up.

"Don't be silly! Of course I wanted to see you—you've been injured. And I'm still mad that I couldn't make your graduation."

"It's fine, Mom. We celebrated with Sierra at Christmas."

"I know, but still. Are you sure you won't come home for the summer?"

Jake shook his head. "You can't take time off work to take care of me. And Andy already has a nurse lined up, so it makes the most sense for us to hang out together. Plus, no one else has to listen to us whine."

"I know. But I worry when you're sick. Make sure you follow the doctor's instructions exactly. God forbid you get an infection or that flesh-eating bug or something like that!"

Jake nodded thoughtfully. "Okay. That hadn't actually occurred to me as a possibility. But thanks for putting it in my head."

"Nom nom nom nom nom." I made chewing noises and held up my mummy hands threateningly.

Sandra's eyes met mine in the rearview mirror. It was a warning look, her mouth pressed tight. I stopped making chewing noises.

"And you, Andy!" she scolded me. "I appreciate your helping us out this summer, but Jake would be in California working by now if not for you."

"Mom!" Jake groaned.

"I know, I know! You said you're responsible for your own decisions, and I agree. But the two of you together are like matches and gasoline, I swear! I hope after this incident, you'll both stop these dangerous tricks. You're lucky you weren't killed!"

"Don't worry, Sandra. I'll be extra good." I made a cross-my-heart gesture with one mummy hand. Which was sort of ironic and funny. I swallowed the smile, though.

"So . . . how's work going?" Jake asked her, no doubt trying to take the pressure off me. Good man.

His mom started talking about her job at the dentist's office, a subject which frequently referred to disgusting procedures and tales of horror. But at least I was forgotten for the moment. I watched the two of them talk, Jake prompting her now and then with a "What happened?" or "Seriously?"

Jake and his mom didn't look much alike. They had the same small, straight nose, but Jake was five eight with an average build. His mom was like five foot nothing. Jake's hair was dark and straight. Hers was dirty blonde and kinky. His eyes were a chocolate brown like liquid Hershey kisses. Hers were a drab blue. He was also a lot smarter than his mom, in the academic sense. Very logical. I figured he'd gotten that from his dad, Mr. Tax Accountant and Serial Monogamist.

"Andy has that all figured out. Don't you, Planinator?"

I blinked and looked at Jake in the front seat of the car. "Huh?"

"I was telling Mom you have everything thought out. How we're going to bathe and eat and all that stuff."

"Pretty much. Of course, Jake is much less dexterous with his toes than I am, so he might have to forego the peanut butter sandwiches."

I was joking. I'd learned a lot at the hospital after just two sessions with a therapist, but very little of it involved toes. The PT person, a chick named Debbie, had known all kinds of tricks, and my dad's super-special insurance had paid for some handy tools from a medical supply place. But, in the hospital, there had always been someone around when I ran into trouble. The nurse would only be at the cottage for a few hours a day. We had some surprises ahead, no doubt.

"Well, I still feel bad leaving you boys on your own in your condition. Promise me if it's not working out, or if you need anything, you'll call me, both of you." Sandra's eyes looked into mine again in the rearview mirror.

"Sure," Jake said.

"Absolutely, Sandra," I agreed.

But we wouldn't. I knew Jake. We could be wallowing on the floor in vomit and our own excrement, covered in sores, and he wouldn't call his mom for help. Because she had "work" and he hated to cause her any trouble. And I wouldn't call her for fear she'd come pick Jake up and I'd never see him again.

I smiled at her reassuringly, though.

It'd be fine. We had each other, and we were smart and creative. Besides, all we really had to do was relax and heal. Just Jake and me. Given the crazy shit we'd done in the past, this had to be a cakewalk.

MAY 2010 - NINTH GRADE
JAKE

I stared at my best friend. "You're insane. Loco! The sanity train has left the station, dude. There's no way I'm doing that!"

Despite my words, I was, in fact, not all that surprised at Andy's suggestion. He had a thing for the bizarre. Recently, he'd made me watch this video of a circus where the performers chewed nails, were lifted by piercings in their back, and put razor blades up their nose and stuff. It was gross. But Andy loved that kind of thing. Street magic too, like David Blaine and Criss Angel. He loved the way people freaked out at that stuff.

But this was one gross-out too far.

He held the box out to me. It was made of clear plastic that was probably specifically designed for insects because there were tiny air holes in the top. Inside were three wiggling green creatures. "Come on! They're perfectly harmless, I swear! Wanna see me eat one?"

"No!"

"So, the trick is to get a bunch of saliva in your mouth," Andy explained patiently, "sort of at the back, like a little well, then open wide, drop it in there, and swallow really fast. You can't even taste it."

"Don't!"

Of course, Andy ignored me. He drew in his cheeks, gathering spit, picked up one of the green, disgusting caterpillars from the box, tilted his head back, opened his mouth, and dropped it in. He gulped quickly. Swallowed again. Then he took a drink from the bottle of water he'd stuck on a nearby half brick wall, grimacing a little. Finally, he looked at me with a big smile even though his eyes were watering. "See? Nothing to it!"

I put my hand over my mouth. "Oh my God, that was *disgusting*. I need to scrub my brain. No, I need an actual lobotomy after seeing that."

"I know!" He grinned excitedly. "Isn't it great? Just imagine how much worse it'll be if people think they're poisonous. They'll go fucking *nuts*!"

This was such a crazy bad idea. It had started when Mr. Bademeyer in biology had brought in some new critters for his tanks. He was into weird life-forms. Come to think of it, Mr. Bademeyer *was* a weird life-form. But, anyway, he had a tarantula, lizards, and other creatures in tanks in his room. Last week he'd added green fuzzy caterpillars from Brazil that he said were the "deadliest caterpillars on earth." They killed a couple of people a year.

After that class, I'd seen a dangerous spark in Andy's eye, and I knew it'd meant trouble. But he hadn't mentioned the caterpillars again until right now.

"Are you sure those aren't actually poisonous? I thought all caterpillars could bite." I eyed the box warily.

"Nah. I got these down by the river, and I Googled them. They're just a garden-variety type. It's really hard to get them to bite you, but even if they did, you might get a little swelling, that's it. And when you swallow 'em fast, they don't have time to bite. I ate two last night and I wasn't nauseous or anything."

"You ate two last night?" I sputtered. "By yourself? What are you, Hannibal the bug cannibal?"

Andy's smile faded and his eyes softened. He punched me lightly in the shoulder. "I had to make sure they weren't dangerous before I talked you into it. You know I'd never hurt you, Jake."

Oh fuck. The bastard. He played me like a snare drum kit. I was so going to give in.

I looked away and stuffed my fists in the pockets of my jeans. It was suddenly awkward. Andy and I didn't say gushy things to each other. Which was probably for the best. Because once I got started, I'd probably never be able to stop.

"So are you in?" Andy urged. "Let's do it at lunch today. It'll be *awesome.*"

"I dunno."

"I dare you. Come on, you saw *me* do it. It's no big deal. Please?"

Of course, I caved in like a cardboard truck run through a car wash.

A few hours later in the lunchroom, I was nervous as hell. I forced myself to eat the corn and hamburger casserole the cafeteria was serving on the theory that it would be better to have food in my stomach for the caterpillar to mix up with than for it to be empty. I only hoped I wasn't going to see that casserole again real soon in the bathroom.

Andy stood up, his chair scraping loudly. A few people looked at him. We were just lowly freshmen at Dunsbar High School, but Andy was popular. His parents had money, he played every sport there was, got good grades, and was stupidly cute on top of all that. As his best friend, I did okay too, even if I wasn't as big on team sports.

He took the little plastic box out of his pocket, held it up with a flourish, and showed it around. The box was clear, so you could see the creepy crawlers in it even from a distance away.

"Oh my God, what is that?" a senior girl said with horror.

"I borrowed a few of the *Lonomia* caterpillars from Mr. Bademeyer's room. Deadliest caterpillars on earth!" Andy announced. He took a step and, with a quick thrust of his arm, showed the box to the girl. She screamed, scrambled out of her chair, and backed away, her face pale.

I hid a smile. Andy was right. This was *awesome*. By now every eye in the cafeteria was fixed on Andy.

"Don't worry," Andy said. "It can't bite you from inside the box. You'd have to hold it or something. Like this." He opened the box, took out one of the bright-green caterpillars, and put it on the back of his hand.

I'd seen the spiky green monsters that Mr. Bademeyer had, and these caterpillars didn't look much like them, but no one seemed to notice or care. Based on the disgust, fear, and horror around the room, everyone was buying it. There were a lot of comments like *Get those things out of here!* And *No way!* And *That is so gross!* There was even a threat to call a teacher, but no one moved to go get one. Andy had chosen his timing well, because I didn't see any of the usual lunchroom monitors.

Andy raised one eyebrow at me. That was my cue. Now more excited than nervous, I stood up and put on a worried face. "Dude! If that thing bites you, you'll be dead in, like, ten minutes. That's what Mr. Bademeyer said."

"Really?" Andy shrugged, examining the caterpillar crawling up his wrist. "I thought that was just, like, old people who could die."

"No, man!" I insisted. "They're more lethal than Cottonmouth snakes! Weren't you listening when he told us about them?"

There was a wave of gasps and groans and, en masse, the entire room of people backed up, trying to get a few inches farther away from Andy and that little green insect. Sheer sadistic delight bubbled up inside me, but I couldn't let it show.

This was *brilliant*! I could tell from the way Andy's eyes shone that he was totally into it too.

"Huh. Dare me to swallow it?" he asked me suddenly.

"What?" I acted surprised.

"Oh, hell no!" some guy muttered in a shocked voice.

"Do you dare me to swallow it?" Andy repeated with a challenge in his voice. "Because I will."

"Andy, don't be an ass!" That was Karen, a freshman cheerleader. A half dozen other kids agreed, telling Andy he was going to hurt himself.

Andy ignored them, staring at me. "Dare me! If I die, I won't blame you. I swear."

That made no sense, but it sounded theatrical. "Yeah, okay. I dare you! Swallow that bad boy. Come on! Do it." I put my hands on my hips and tilted up my chin, egging him on.

"I will . . . but only if you do it too." Andy held out the box to me. "Dare you."

I tried to look cornered and like I was pretending to be brave even though I was scared. Oscar material, man. I took the box, my hand shaking only a little. Okay. Here was the not-so-fun part. But, honestly, with everyone staring at us, horrified and fascinated, some laughing, some with hands plastered over their mouths, eyes wide, it was surprisingly not that awful. What was swallowing a bug compared to that kind of attention? Hell, even the seniors were completely hooked. And people ate way grosser things on reality TV shows all the time.

I opened the box and started gathering saliva in the back of my mouth. *Oh my God. I can't believe I'm doing this.*

Andy brushed his caterpillar into his palm and held it up to his mouth. "Ready? One. Two . . ."

I put the second caterpillar in my hand, preparing to pinch it with two fingers and toss it down.

Andy's blue eyes, bright as rocket flares, stared into mine. I could do anything when he looked at me like that. I could fucking *fly*. My heart jackhammered in my chest.

"Three!"

We tossed them down.

Chapter

FIVE

Those first few days at the Osterville cottage, learning how to function without hands, were so frustrating. I couldn't have coped if it had been just me. I would have been pissed off and depressed, a broody bastard, that was for sure. But I wasn't alone. Andy was right there with me, and he managed to make it ridiculous, and dorky, and even hilarious at times.

Shortly after my mom "got us settled" and left that first day, we wanted a beer. There was a six-pack with twist-off tops in the fridge, and Andy and I took turns trying to get the damn bottle caps off. We could move the bottles around by gripping them with our wrists, but we couldn't get the caps off. We spent our first hour alone at the cabin trying and failing. I held the bottle between my knees while Andy tried to twist the cap with his elbows and then wrists, but it didn't work. He couldn't get enough of a grip. He wanted to try his toes, but I wasn't having any part of that. He hopped around the kitchen chasing me until we were howling with laughter.

We finally figured out if one of us could grip the bottle hard enough with his wrists, the other could twist the cap off with his teeth most of the time, unless the cap was particularly stubborn. By the time we got two bottles open, we were sweaty and exhausted from laughing so much.

Everything, every stupid little thing, was a total pain in the ass like that. But Andy took each problem as a challenge. He'd get that focused look, lick his lips, and try to figure out how to get it done by any means. He wasn't afraid of looking ridiculous, or crossing a line, or being disgusting. He cracked me the hell up. I could tell he was being over-the-top crazy on purpose. Like he was trying to cheer me up, take my mind off the pain that still radiated through my hands, and off the sheer hellacious inconvenience, my delayed job start, and everything else.

I appreciated that. I really did. There was no one else I'd rather be in a shit situation with. Andy made it all bearable. And that made me think about how, over the years, Andy had made a lot of things bearable for me. Issues with kids at school. My worry over grades and money. The way my dad had left us.

Fuck. That still hurt. I didn't want to think about that.

Over the first few days, we figured out the basics needed to survive. We had help. Emily was a cute redhead in her late twenties, married, and a bit motherly. She came over to the cabin in the morning and made us breakfast. She left us food for the whole day in containers covered with foil wrap that was easy to nudge off. Andy had gotten us these tools that clamped around our forearms and had stiff plastic arms. On the end you could attach various little gadgets, like a spoon, and that was how we ate. Emily also left large travel mugs filled with iced tea and lemonade, complete with straws. She did the dishes and laundry, made our beds, and picked up the place. Usually we had a list of things we wanted her or Bob to do that we couldn't manage, things like changing batteries in the remote, opening a window, or moving the chairs on the dock.

Then there was Walter, our nurse. He came at ten every morning, about the time Emily left. He gave Andy and me a shower—separately, of course—and got us dressed. He shaved us, changed our bandages, checked the burns, and put antibiotic ointment and numbing cream on our hands. He laid out fresh clothes for later in case we wanted them. He fed us our daily antibiotic and checked our pain meds. After the first few days, I was down to one Vicodin before bed and prescription-strength aspirin the rest of the time. I hated feeling spaced out, but the pain was bad enough that I couldn't sleep without help.

By 11 a.m., Walter was gone, and it was just Andy and me. We had our phones in case we needed help fast. Siri could dial anyone by name. But we never called anyone. We got by on our own.

I shouldn't have liked that as much as I did. But, honestly, it was nice. The weather was gorgeous, that rare perfection of late May when the days were sunny and warm without being humid and stinking hot. There was a breeze over the sound that ruffled our hair as we sat out on the dock in folding chairs. The cottage was on a little cove, so there wasn't a ton of traffic, just a motorboat or small yacht now and then. The water was usually quiet and peaceful.

I'd always loved the cottage. I mean, who wouldn't? It wasn't a huge mansion like some places along the shore, but it had blue shingles with white trim, a cute-as-fuck front entrance with a vine-covered overhang, three bedrooms, and a bright kitchen with white cupboards and a big window that overlooked the water. The pine furniture was supposed to look rustic and "cabin-like," but it probably cost a mint. There were plaid fabrics everywhere, a woodstove, and a big-screen TV.

Not that Andy and I had spent much time in the cottage. We were always on the water, or at least we had been before this trip. They owned a canoe and a speedboat, jet skis, and any other water toy you could possibly want. Andy and I had come down here a lot in middle school and high school and hung out, spending all day playing on the sound. But I'd only been here twice since we'd started college. It was a five-hour drive from NYU, and my summers had been spent working in Boston, trying to sock away as much money as possible. There'd been hardly any downtime.

So to be here in Cape Cod, just Andy and me, with nothing to do except appreciate the fucking amazing scenery and rest, was actually pretty sweet. Neverware had agreed to move my start date to September first, and they'd been really nice about it, even sending me a get-well card. So I couldn't complain. It was a free vacation, and after busting my ass for the past four years, it was nice to just chill for a while. As long as my hands healed without any permanent damage, I figured I was ahead.

Except—there wasn't a whole lot we could do. We couldn't get in the water, because the doctor didn't want us exposing the burns to the salt water. God only knew what was in there, what with all the Canadian geese and boat motor fuel and pollution. If I was going to pick up a flesh-eating bacteria anywhere, it would be in that water. We couldn't manage the boats by ourselves either. We couldn't play b-ball, tennis, or even badminton without fucking up our hands. Andy was a sports fanatic though, so we spent hours lazily kicking a soccer ball around on the green lawn that ran between the cottage and the dock. We couldn't run because our hands would start to hurt—probably because of the blood pressure or just the jarring motion. But we took long walks along the beach or around the shoreline neighborhood to a local park.

When Andy would let me sit still for a while, I could get by on my computer, phone, and Kindle using voice commands and light taps with the tip of my bandaged hand. Thank God for accessibility. But it was too cumbersome to spend hours writing or surfing the web.

Mostly, we sat on the deck, sunbathed, and talked. At first my mind was restless. I was used to being constantly bombarded with demands and distractions and shit I had to get done. But Andy was chill, and by the third day, fuck, so was I. It felt wonderful. It felt like I'd been on a rocket for the past four years and hadn't even realized it. It was such a relief to just slow down.

Slow down—and hang with Andy. When was the last time Andy and I had just hung out together and done nothing? Sure, we'd roomed together all through college, and we'd watch movies sometimes, or go out together on a Saturday night. But we'd both been so busy we'd rarely had a whole day together. I'd worked twenty hours a week at the language center as well as taken at least sixteen hours in credits. And Andy had been busy with his pre-law classes and girlfriends.

But now, with our bandaged hands, no school, work a distant cloud on the horizon, and no friends or girlfriends or family around, we only had each other. I liked it. Probably too much. There was no use in getting more attached to Andy than I already was. We'd be living on opposite sides of the continent soon. And I'd started to disengage myself emotionally years ago—had to. But being at the shore reminded me of how it felt to just exist in Andy's space. It was as though there was a positive energy current between us, like two poles that magnetically attracted and boosted each other to a higher level.

It was just *good mojo* to be with him. I'd almost forgotten how warm and amazing it felt, why we were best friends in the first place, why I'd never been able to pull free from his orbit.

"Tell me what the campus is like at Harvard. You've been there, right?" I asked on our third afternoon at the shore. We were sitting on the dock in two lawn chairs.

He nodded. "Yeah. My dad and I swung by last summer when I was making my final decision. But, actually, we went to see it years ago."

"Yeah?" My chair was near the edge of the dock, and I trailed my toe in the water.

Andy cleared his throat like he was about to go into a story. "Yeah. When I was twelve, I guess it was just before we met, my dad took me on a road trip over a long weekend. We visited MIT, Yale, Harvard, NYU, and a couple of other schools."

"You never told me about that." I wasn't surprised though. Andy's father was the ultimate stage dad, only in his case, it was all about schools and his career. "Holding out on me. That is so secret agent of you."

Andy chuckled. "Oh yeah. It was very secret agent-y. Seriously, Dad made a booklet with the features of each school along with their ranking stats in medicine, law, business, engineering, and finance. It was pretty impressive. The campuses. The buildings. The pomp and circumstance. Especially when I was twelve."

"No shit." Even the name *Harvard* impressed me, and I was twenty-two years old. I could imagine what Andy must have thought at age twelve. I was proud as hell of him for having been accepted there.

"It was a good weekend," Andy mused. "Just . . . thinking about all the possibilities. Getting excited about it. Hanging out with my dad. Feeling all grown-up. You know? Oh, and we went to a football game at MIT. That was sick."

I felt a twinge of jealousy. My dad had never spent that kind of time with me when I was a kid, and then he'd left us entirely. "I still think you should have played some football at NYU. You would have loved it."

Andy only shrugged. "Nah. I wasn't good enough to have a shot at the pros, and as a casual thing, college football wasn't worth it. Too much risk of injury and too much time taken away from my studies."

It was weird. Sometimes I could practically hear Andy's dad talking through Andy's mouth. I decided to drop the football topic. "So you liked Harvard the best then, even on that trip?"

He leaned back in his chair, all loose-limbed and sprawling. His eyes were closed and covered with sunglasses, face tilted to the sun. Not that I was looking. "I don't remember having a strong opinion at the time. The schools were all impressive. Though I liked NYU the least. All the traffic and inner-city stuff." He smiled at the irony.

Yeah. NYU had been overwhelming to me too, the first time I'd seen it. Still, I wouldn't trade my four years there for anything.

"Wish you were going with me to Harvard," Andy said, out of the blue. His voice was serious.

I gave that a moment of due consideration. I would have loved to get a master's in computer science at a school like Harvard, but I didn't have wealthy parents to pay my way. "Yeah, well. Not all of us can be *you*, all Damien Thorn and everything."

"Shut up. Still wish you were going."

Andy's voice was sincere. I felt a tightening in my chest. Was he saying he'd miss me? I gave him a nudge with my elbow, then drew it back onto the arm of my chair. He nudged me back and left his elbow on my armrest, just barely touching me.

A swamping heat blossomed in my stomach, and it had nothing to do with the sun.

Damn. I wasn't supposed to be sitting here on Nantucket Sound with my best friend and getting all wistful about us. I was supposed to be starting a new job in California, a new life, my adult life. I was moving on.

"Name ten things you're looking forward to the most in California," Andy prompted me in an upbeat tone. I swore, sometimes it was like he could read my mind.

I settled back with a sigh. "Right. Um. The happy cows? Isn't that a thing?"

"Dude. Seriously."

I rolled my eyes. "The beach?"

"You gonna learn to surf?" Andy sounded eager. If he were the one moving to California, he'd be on a surfboard by the end of the first week.

"Maybe once I get settled into my job and apartment and all that. Locate a laundromat. Adopt a stray cat. But Cupertino isn't that close to the ocean, you know. I think it's at least forty-five minutes away."

"Huh. That sucks. Why even be in California if you're not on the ocean?"

"A question I ask myself nightly," I deadpanned. In truth, I didn't care all that much. I'd be working long hours anyway.

"Well, what are you looking forward to, then?"

"Having a desk and my own computer at work. My first official work space."

"Nerd."

"You know it."

"What else?"

"Finding an apartment. Setting it up." I'd be living with Sierra at first. But I looked forward to getting my own space once I had a few paychecks under my belt.

"Okay. That's two."

"Sun, baby. Perpetual sun." I taunted him. Harvard was close to Boston, and we both knew what that climate was like.

"Fucker. That's three."

"Getting to know people at work. Maybe I'll make some new friends. Find a new drug dealer. Join a cult."

Andy huffed a laugh. "Yeah. Because that's so you. That's four. What else?"

I thought about it. "Exploring the state. State parks. Hiking trails and shit. Seeing San Francisco." That would be more fun to do with Andy there. But Andy wouldn't be there. And I *would* make new friends, I reminded myself.

"Five."

I shifted in my chair. "I guess California's supposed to be liberal. I'm looking forward to being in that kind of environment. More diversity and all." I talked around what I really meant. I hadn't been honest with Andy about certain things in the past, and I wasn't going to tell him now. So I kept it vague.

But Andy pressed the issue. "More diversity? There's a lot of diversity at NYU."

"That's true." I changed the subject. "Let's see. That was six. Um ... Mexican food? I hear they have killer Mexican food there. And not frozen burritos by the pound either."

Andy scoffed. "You're down to the food already? What about California girls? I would have thought they'd be number one."

"Right. California girls," I agreed.

I was looking forward to that, sort of. I knew there would be lots of beautiful girls in California, but I was uneasy about whether or not I'd get on with any of them. Would they be beautiful but shallow like in the movies? Would I meet someone I had anything in common with? Or maybe I'd find a different sort of connection.

"Having sex in your own place without your roommate barging in," Andy suggested.

"Oh, yeah! That's eight, nine, and ten," I joked.

He laughed and leaned forward to drink from his straw. Our lawn chairs had cup holders, which was convenient for those of us without palms, and Emily had made us big cooler glasses of iced tea.

His elbow dug into me a little more with his shift in position. My gaze was drawn to his pursed lips around the straw. That punch-drunk band of butterflies came back.

Fuck, Andy was so gorgeous. It was unfair to us mere mortals, and sometimes it hit me in the solar plexus from out of nowhere. If anyone had seen me, I'd probably have looked like a kid gazing at Santa Claus, my eyes glowing with rapturous awe. It was embarrassing.

He'd always been thin and lanky and tall. His hair was naturally a dirty blond, but he'd bleached it nearly white for a punk phase in high school, and it looked so great on him he'd kept it. He had cheekbones for days and a jawline so sharp it could put your eye out. The best part was his eyes though. They were light blue, usually soft and amused, and when the sunlight shone in them, they could steal a little bit of your soul. Even when he was being a brat, he was just ... a gravitational force. He was good the way rambunctious dogs were good. Or hyper babies. Or the Energizer Bunny.

I'd never find another friend like him. Not in California. Not in the world. But then, maybe that was for the best. Being friends with Andy had its own pain, and it had nothing to do with his stunts.

I closed my eyes and focused on feeling the sun on my upturned face. My hands weren't in as much agony as they'd been at the start, but they throbbed right now, the nerves pulsing like silent voodoo drums. Maybe that was the skin healing. The Vicodin from last night had worn off and the mega aspirin wasn't strong enough to make me stoned, but the sound of lapping water and the sun on my face allowed my brain to slip into a relaxed zone easier than it otherwise might have done.

"Tell me a ghost story." Andy sounded as drowsy as I felt.

I smiled. We used to love to stay up late and tell ghost stories. Jesus, those were the days. "It's too bright out here to set the right atmosphere."

"Don't care."

Neither did I. We could both close our eyes and pretend. "Okay. So one night this guy takes his girl out onto a country road to make out . . ."

Chapter
SIX

JUNE 2017
ANDY

The first few weeks at the cottage we had good weather and spent most of our time outside. Walter said our burns were coming along well. So far we'd avoided making things worse, which was a miracle. The burns were gnarly looking though, and painful when he rewrapped them.

My palms were the bright red of fresh blood. They looked like they'd been dipped in boiling water, with layers around the edge turning white and loose in spots. My hands alternated between a mild burning and piercing pain that went supernova anytime I accidentally clenched them or bumped them into something. Doing or lifting anything that required any pressure on the skin whatsoever was right out.

So by the time we'd been basking on the Nantucket Sound for two weeks, I was climbing the fucking walls.

"I've never been this damn horny in my life," I complained to Jake, bitterly and sincerely.

It was almost noon, and we were sitting out on the dock like we usually did. It had been great hanging out together. We'd caught up on a lot of stuff we never seemed to get around to talking about during school—his upcoming new life. Harvard. Our mutual friends and exes. We'd told ghost stories. We'd taken long walks and kicked around a soccer ball for hours. We'd played poker on Jake's tablet and consumed six seasons of *The Walking Dead* on the big-screen TV. It was nice having undivided Jake time, but I'd reached the point where frustration had me close to tears.

Not tears of boredom either. Sexually frustrated tears.

"Turn page," Jake responded. He was reading on his Kindle.

"I'm not sure how that would help me get off," I joked.

Jake snorted, but he didn't rise to the bait.

I shifted in my chair. I wasn't kidding. I couldn't remember the last time I'd gone more than two days without an orgasm. Probably not since I'd figured out the magical wonderland that was my dick when I was eleven years old. I'd had a permanent semi for days now, and my loose, silky gym shorts—worn because I could get them up and down by myself if I scooched against a wall—were doing nothing to disguise it or help it go away.

I moved my bandaged hands onto the arms of the deck chair and looked down at myself. Even looking at my crotch made my dick grow under the silky blue fabric. It was like a hopeful puppy anticipating attention.

In my peripheral vision, I saw Jake glance at it too. He leaned forward in his chair, hunching toward the Kindle, which was propped on a little table in front of him. "Turn page."

"You did not just read an entire page." I smirked.

"Shut up, Mr. TMI." Jake fake-read some more.

But I knew I had his attention. "Have you figured out a way to get off yet? Because I haven't."

"No," he said in a distracted voice. Despite his blasé look, I knew there was no way he was absorbing a single word on that Kindle screen.

"Me neither. I tried humping the bed, but it didn't work. Fucking mattress is so soft and lumpy."

"Can you not give me the gory details?" Jake hunched further and stared at the Kindle.

"Rubbing against the tiles in the shower didn't work. They're too hard."

He snorted. "What are you, the Goldilocks of self-love?"

I chuckled. "That's me. I need something *just right*." I used a filthy voice on the last bit.

Jake shifted uneasily but didn't look at me. "Too bad Amber dumped you. Maybe you could call her and play the poor invalid card. She might be willing to drive down for a conjugal visit."

"Nah. So not worth the bowing and scraping I'd have to do."

I gave it a moment, trying to build up my nerve.

I hadn't been kidding. I'd tried a half-dozen ways to get off, but nothing was working. So I'd put some serious brain power into figuring out a solution. I was good at working around obstacles, but the obvious answer—the thing I really *wanted*—involved Jake, and I wasn't sure how he'd react.

Just thinking about it, I plumped up further, causing a definite tent in my shorts. I half expected Jake to tease me, something like, *You could poke someone's eye out with that thing.*

But all he said was, "Turn page."

"So . . . you haven't gotten off since before the hospital?" I asked.

"*No,*" Jake said quickly. "And it's not helping to talk about it, thank you very much. It's like when you talk about having a tickle in your throat, it makes you want to cough." His voice was tense. I saw his eyes flicker toward my shorts, though he didn't turn his head and he continued to pretend to read.

My heart pounded. I felt exposed at the moment, my semi obscene, so I sat up and hunched forward too, elbows on my knees. I watched a ski boat go by. The roar of the motor was loud. I waited until it had passed. Then I swallowed and told myself it didn't matter. It was no big deal to suggest it. And if he said no, it was no biggie. I could play it off as a joke. But it really didn't feel that way.

"Speaking of a tickle in your throat . . . I have an idea about how we can get off."

"You do?" Jake's tone was fast and curious. Definitely interested.

"Yup."

"Like what? Gonna have Walter install a Fleshlight in the shower?" He chuckled.

I huffed. "Yeah. You know my dad combs through every one of my credit card statements. No way am I ordering a Fleshlight. Not to mention the fact that I'd have to kill myself after asking Walter to install something like that."

Walter, our nurse, was in his fifties, white, bald, and pudgy. He had a squeaky-clean fundamentalist thing going on and had mentioned "praying" for us several times. Ix-nay on asking Walter to mount a fuck tube in the shower.

"So what then, Oh Planinator?" Jake sat up from his slouch and looked at me.

Unable to meet his gaze, I studied the water. "Okay, so just hear me out before saying no."

"Oh shit. You only say that when it's *really* whacked."

"Come on! I'm serious."

Jake sighed, but I could swear there was a new tension in the air. He was no longer pretending to read his Kindle. He leaned back in his chair and waited. "Go on, then. Spit it out."

I grinned and turned my head to look at him, raising an eyebrow. "That's the goal, yeah."

He kicked my leg lightly with his bare heel. "Just say it."

"Okay. So. We can't jerk off, right?" I held up my bandaged hands a little.

"Obviously."

"Well, have you ever heard of guys who can, you know, suck their own dicks?"

There was a sharp inhale from Jake, but he kept his face blank. "Yeah. I can't though. Not even a little bit."

"I know. Me neither. So I thought . . ." Fuck. This was hard to say. Incredibly hard to say. But there was no point in beating around the bush. "Okay. So. What if we sucked each other, like, at the same time, and *pretended* we were doing ourselves? Sort of self-suck by proxy."

I'd intended to keep a jokey tone during this, so I could claim I was teasing. But the words started tumbling out, and there was a hollow ringing in my ears. I honestly didn't have the slightest fucking clue what my tone had been or how it must have sounded to Jake.

Next to me, he went deadly still. He stared down at his knees. There was a little frown behind his brow. He looked worried. Or disturbed. Or both concurrently.

I fought the urge to overexplain or justify. *Play it cool.* I leaned back in my chair and closed my eyes as if soaking in the sun. "It would get the job done." I shrugged.

"Did you honestly just ask me to suck you off?" Jake asked in a quiet voice.

"No. That's not what I said. Don't go all homophobic on me, bro. Look, we can't use our hands at all. Fact. If you *could* suck yourself, you would—right? Fact. But you can't. I'm in the same boat. So I'm thinking if we were end to end, we could close our eyes and pretend we're doing ourselves. And we'd get off. And we wouldn't have to get Walter or anyone else involved. It's really the best solution."

Jake was silent again for a long moment. "I'm not doing that." His voice was firm, grim, like he meant it.

Honestly, I was surprised. And a little hurt.

"Fine," I said. "It was just a suggestion. You got a better idea? Or do you want the worst case of blue balls ever? Because I'm about to crawl the fucking walls."

"I'm not doing it," he repeated adamantly.

"Yeah, I heard you the first time, Jake."

In my peripheral vision, I could see he was stiff and tense, like he might bolt. But, finally, he relaxed. He leaned forward toward the Kindle. "Turn page," he said, his voice tight.

"What if I dared you?" I asked, unable to let it go.

"Jesus, Andy, fuck off!" Jake snarled. He got up and stormed toward the cottage. We'd figured out that if we kicked the bottom of the screen door, it would bounce open for a second, long enough to get one foot in. He did this harder than necessary and went inside. I was so shocked, I let him go without a word.

Goddamn it. I'd known it would be risky to bring it up, but some part of me believed Jake would jump at the chance. Or, worst case, brush it off as a joke. I hadn't expected anger. Jake had never told me to fuck off like that. Not that I could remember.

Shit.

Okay. Bad idea. Abort, abort. But it was too late to take it back.

Chapter SEVEN

JAKE

I stormed into the cottage and went straight through the living room to the bathroom. The door was open, so I went in and bumped the door shut hard with my hip, not even caring that it would be difficult to open it again. I slid down the wall and sat on the floor.

I needed to get away from Andy, at least for a few minutes. Here at the cottage, like in our dorm room at school, getting away from Andy was nearly impossible. If he wasn't actually in the room, his presence still flooded everything, larger than life, like the sun I revolved around. Normally, I was fine with that. But, at the moment, it was too much.

Holy Mother of God and Baby Jesus, Andy just suggested we sixty-nine to get each other off. I was completely losing it. My stomach was knotted and aching. My heart pounded in my ears. I couldn't even tell what emotion I was feeling. Outrage? Fear? Desire? Shock?

Shock, I decided. It was definitely plain-old, run-of-the-mill shock.

I sat there for an unknown amount of time with my eyes closed, trying to get it to sink in. And, finally, logic began to trickle back into my brain like a stream only temporarily diverted from its course.

You know Andy. This is just an expedient solution, like the tools from medical supply. It means nothing to him one way or the other.

Yeah. I got that. Or I thought I did. But, even so, I was surprised that Andy would be willing to suck another guy off for any reason.

Even if the favor was returned. Even if he had no other way to get off. The *idea* of Andy doing that, being okay with that, even in a hetero "whatever, it's no worse than eating bugs" kind of way, was bewildering to me. Because I'd always assumed, told myself, that Andy would never do that. Never want to. Never would. Period.

But you know Andy. He'll do anything.

Yeah. That was true. Andy was an adrenaline junkie, the biggest shock jock I knew. But there was "anything" when it came to stupid stuff like sticking something in a light socket, chewing an entire jalapeño, licking a frozen metal pole, or jumping his dirt bike over the quarry. And then there was "anything" when it came to fooling around with guys. Despite knowing Andy was the poster boy for the former, I'd never thought he'd go near the latter.

It was freaking me the fuck out. I'd kept a secret from him, from my best friend in all the world, and this stupid idea of his threatened to expose everything, in more ways than one. Here was the thing I had never told Andy: I was bisexual. While Andy had only seen me date girls, I was also attracted to certain guys. And I'd followed up on that. I'd had sex with men. Well, with one guy anyway.

Because I couldn't tell Andy about that, and Andy and I had pretty much the same circle of friends, I didn't tell anyone. Except my sister. She knew. And, of course, the guy I'd been with.

I wasn't ashamed of it or in denial. I wasn't intentionally hiding in the closet. I was cool with the entire LGBTQ rainbow. It was just . . . I didn't want Andy to know about me. I *really* didn't want Andy to know. The thought of him knowing made me feel sweaty and nauseous. Sort of like I was feeling right now.

It wasn't that Andy was a homophobe, or that I thought he'd hate me. We had a friend, Cody, who was openly gay, and Andy had never treated him any differently than anyone else. I'd never heard him talk smack about gay people.

But Cody hadn't grown up with Andy. He hadn't spent at least one night a week in Andy's bed from eighth grade on. I was afraid if Andy knew I was bisexual, he'd be wondering if I'd thought about him like that, if I'd lusted after him when we'd showered together in the locker room or when we'd been in our underwear sharing covers.

He'd wonder if I'd wanted him, how badly, and for how long. He'd wonder if I'd had a massive crush on him all these years.

How could he *not* think those things? Andy was a good-looking guy. Everyone found him attractive. If I was into men, why wouldn't I want him? Why wouldn't I think about touching him? About grazing my hand over his back when we played one-on-one basketball and his shirt was off and his skin was pale and sweaty. Why wouldn't I think about rolling closer to him in the night just to learn how the length of his body felt against mine? To check out the size and shape of his morning wood? Why wouldn't I wonder what it would be like to kiss him?

Why wouldn't I be in love with him?

Nope. I didn't want Andy to know I was bisexual. That would reveal a whole murky hidden pool of stuff I couldn't bear for him to know about. That stuff was my secret pain or buried sin or whatever, and I was taking it to the grave. Also, there was no way him knowing wouldn't change our friendship. Not that Andy would ditch me immediately. But. Maybe the Andy and Jake Show would slowly dissolve, eaten away by awkwardness. It was true, we were going to be apart soon anyway. But that made me even more determined to keep things unchanged between us for as long as possible. I'd held my secrets for this long. I wanted to go out with honor.

Even more important than my honor was my sanity. I'd struggled with my feelings for years. I'd put myself through *so* much torture in the past. I'd finally gotten to a good place with it. I was fine now. I'd compartmentalized. I'd moved on. We were still friends, best friends, but I had emotional distance these days. I had a life full of other things. I didn't pine for Andy anymore.

Now he wanted to suck each other off? Because it was an easy mechanical solution to a logistical problem? No. No way. I'd never be able to keep my past feelings a secret if we did that. Not to mention the fact that getting my hands—or mouth—on Andy for real would probably trigger another four to five years of unrequited hell. I was like an addict who'd finally gotten clean. I wasn't going to do that to myself again.

Even if the idea of being sexual with Andy in the real world—like, it *actually* happening—was unbearably tempting. Even though I'd never reneged on a dare. I wasn't doing this.

Goddamn it, Andy. I wanted to hate him. I really did.

ANDY

So. That'd been a massive fuckup. Jake barely talked to me for the rest of the day. He took a long walk without asking if I wanted to go along. And when he got back, he stayed glued to his Kindle.

We didn't talk about it. I didn't know what else to say. Seemed like any way I tried to minimize it, play it off as no big deal, would only make it a bigger deal. I couldn't see why Jake was so upset in the first place. All he had to do was say no. I knew for a fact he wasn't as inexperienced as he was pretending to be. Why was he acting so pissed off?

It frustrated me. And it stung too. So we both just didn't talk about it. We moved around each other in the microcosm of the cottage and pretended nothing was wrong.

I should never have suggested it, but it'd seemed like the perfect opportunity to figure some things out. Things that had been bothering me for a long time. See, the real problem began with Kevin.

It happened last year, the fall semester of our junior year. One weekend in October, I had to go home to Boston because it was my mom's birthday. She was being honored by some professional women's association, and she wanted me and my dad at the awards dinner.

My mom's family was Jewish, though non-practicing. My dad was raised Protestant or something like that, but he wasn't religious now. Mom's a lawyer, crazy smart. She worked for a big law firm in Boston doing corporate law, but her passion was her pro bono stuff, usually cases involving women—sexual harassment, wrongful termination, pregnant women's rights in prison, whatever. She worked *all the time*. When I'd been younger, I'd resented it. I'd felt as though my mom was so focused on helping total strangers that she didn't have time for her own kid. Sometimes I'd thought that if I had been born a girl, it would have been different. My mom was so into women's issues. But because I was a boy, and not abused or in prison, I didn't register to her. It was fucked up, I knew. I didn't really think that anymore. I guessed she was just into what she was into.

Anyway, that weekend, I woke up Sunday morning after her awards dinner and just couldn't hang around at home anymore. I was in the car by 7 a.m. to drive the four hours back to campus. Jake wasn't expecting me back so early. When I tried to go into our dorm room, I found the door locked. I figured Jake had gone somewhere and locked the door, so I dug out my key.

"Who is it?" I heard Jake call from inside the room.

"It's me, genius. Open the door."

"Hang on."

I heard banging and whispers. I leaned against the wall and waited, grinning. So Jake had picked up a girl. Nice. He'd been studying too hard. There was only one other time I'd been cast out of the room by the proverbial sock on the door—and that was because of Jeanette, a Jake girlfriend that had lasted a few months our freshman year.

But when the door opened, Jake walked out with his coat on, and following him was a guy.

"Hey," Jake said casually, slinging his backpack over his shoulder. "You're back early."

"Yeah. Um. Decided to get back." I glanced at the guy. I'd never seen him before. He had longish dark hair, a bit of acne, pale-blue eyes. He was a hipster type. He wore a navy sweater and jeans. There was a humorous look in his eyes as he stared at me, like he thought something was funny.

"Oh, um, Kevin, this is my roommate, Andy. Andy, this is Kevin. He's in comp sci too."

"Hey, Kevin," I said.

"Hey, Andy." Kevin bit his lips like he was trying not to smile. He looked down at the floor, his lips twisting wryly.

I gave Jake a look—*What the hell is going on?* He ignored it, but he had a manic glint in his eye and a red blotch on his neck like he was nervous. "We were just heading to the library to study. See ya." They left.

I went into the room, shaking my head.

Jake's bed had been hastily made. The room smelled like sex. Like *serious* come-smell. I opened a window. I grunted a *huh,* dropped my bag, and sat on my bed, thinking about it.

Had Jake really been having sex with a guy? Minutes ago? In this very room? It sure looked and smelled that way.

Was Jake *gay*? If so, why had he never told me?

But the more I thought about it, the more I had a hard time believing that. I'd seen Jake with girls. I'd seen Jake *making out* with girls. We'd traded porn links. I knew about the folder he had on his hard drive with pictures of Jaclyn Swedberg, a brunette-and-brainy Playboy Playmate. I'd witnessed his legit crush on May Alderson our senior year. I was ninety-nine percent sure all of that hadn't been faked.

So not totally gay, then. Was he just experimenting? Had he decided to try gay sex for the hell of it? Or was he bi or pan or something I didn't even have a term for?

I had no clue. Later that night, when Jake got back, I asked him about Kevin. He gave me a long-winded explanation about them being in his components class together and how they were working on a project. Since he was obviously going out of his way not to admit it—*hey, Andy, I had sex with that guy*—I let it go.

Jake never brought Kevin back to our room again. They went . . . somewhere. Jake admitted he was going out to "study with Kevin," avoiding my eyes when he said it. A few times he stayed out all night, claiming he'd slept on Kevin's couch. And I never said, "So how is the gay sex, then, Jakey?"

I didn't understand, though. Why Kevin? What was so special about him? And why wouldn't Jake tell me? It bugged me. It bugged *the shit* out of me. It got to the point where any time Jake said he was going to study with Kevin, I wanted to hit something. Jake's girlfriends had never felt threatening to me, but Kevin did. He could be everything to Jake—friend and bed bunny, lover and someone to hang out with. He could give Jake something I couldn't, and I didn't like it.

I wasn't sorry when, about a month later, Jake casually mentioned they weren't hanging out anymore. I literally went into the hall and did a little victory jump and high five. I wasn't proud of it.

Ever since then, things had gotten more and more twisted up in my head. It was like that old story about opening Pandora's box and not being able to put the stuff back inside and close the lid again. For as long as I could remember, I would sometimes look at Jake, in some random moment, like in the hall in high school when he was leaning down to get a drink of water from the fountain, and I'd have a little reaction in my belly and, farther down, that little thrill. And I'd be like, *Wtf, man. That's* Jake!

As the years went by, I wrote it off as a horny-guy thing. Or maybe a cross-wiring thing because we were so close. There was no one I was closer to than Jake, and no person I liked as much, not even the girls I dated. Especially not the girls I dated. So I figured it was natural to feel "a little bit of something" like that, even though that wasn't what I *really* wanted. It was like getting an urge to eat a yummy-looking piece of cake, even if you weren't hungry, even if you didn't like cake all that much.

Because even if I *liked* cake—even if I *loved* it, and I didn't—cake was bad for me. I wasn't gay, and I didn't want to be. I liked girls. My future life made way more sense with a house and a wife and kids and all of that. And, besides, Jake had showed no interest in that either when we'd been in high school. He liked girls. And that was that.

Until Kevin. The thing with Kevin had flicked some switch in my brain, opened up new possibilities. When Jake came back from the showers and was standing there looking through his closet wearing a towel, or when he was asleep on his bed with the covers off wearing only briefs, I'd look at him and think, *He had sex with a guy.* My imagination would start trying to picture it. Jake with a guy. Jake naked. Jake having sex—with another hard body.

A few months later, after the Kevin thing, Jake started dating Kimmy, a cute, smart-mouthed Asian girl who was a journalism major. He was obviously really into her, at least until she transferred to London and they decided not to do the long-distance thing.

So.

I'd thought I'd get over the whole Kevin thing. I hadn't. I still thought about it—about Jake and Kevin. About Jake and guys.

About Jake and me.

If he was bisexual, why had he never tried it on with me? Hell, we'd never even wanked in the same room, nothing like the stories some guys told. We didn't even really talk about sex that much. If I so much as mentioned jerking off, Jake always got quiet and didn't reply, like he was uncomfortable. I figured he was a bit of a prude. It made sense—Jake was so serious about things.

Now here we were, stuck together for the summer. All summer. Our last summer. Our last summer *ever*.

Why did I suggest the mutual-blowjobs thing? It absolutely made sense, problem-solving wise. And once I'd thought about it, I liked the idea more and more. Because it was a chance—a chance to try it out, sex with Jake, without it being a huge deal. I'd never experimented with a guy. What if I really wasn't into dick? What if I hated it? It was like taking your first bite of yogurt, you know? I didn't want to start something with Jake and then not be able to do it, hurt his feelings or piss him off. If we did it like this, as a mechanical solution to a problem, it would be easy to shrug it off as a short-term thing if I couldn't do it.

Besides, it was the last chance. If it didn't happen this summer, it never would. And that idea made me feel a little wild. I was getting that itchy urge inside me, the one that insisted I do something risky, cross a line, cross a dozen.

But, apparently, even when I handed my dick to Jake on a silver platter, he didn't want me. He'd wanted Kevin, but not me.

Okay. At least now I knew.

Chapter
EIGHT

ANDY

I woke up Monday morning hard as an iron post, the kind they put up in Boston to make sure cars didn't enter pedestrian zones. I'd been dreaming about sex, though I couldn't remember the details. God *damn*, but I had to get off. I was becoming seriously irritable, especially being around Jake all the time. He could have ended this so easily, not only the physical torment itself, but the questions that were starting to drive me crazy. And yet he hadn't even acknowledged I'd suggested we get each other off since he'd first walked away on Friday morning.

Fine! I'd figure out another way to do it, then.

I went into the bathroom. It was too difficult to turn the lock on the door and, anyway, if Jake walked in on me, that was his problem. I couldn't even piss with my aching hard-on, and I was so done with this. The sink in the bathroom was free-standing and had a curved porcelain edge. It was at the right height that I figured I might be able to rub off against it. Of course, cold porcelain wasn't exactly conducive to comfort. I bent over and grasped a towel off the rack with my teeth. I tried to drape it over the basin. What I wanted was a clean double fold so there would be two thickness of terrycloth between me and the porcelain. But the towel dropped twice, forcing me to get onto my knees to pick it back up in my teeth and use my elbows to get back on my feet. Then I could only get a single layer of the towel in place, despite spending ages trying to fold it with my elbows.

Finally I gave up and just tried to rub off against it, but the surface was still too hard. And it was bunched up all wrong, making uncomfortable folds. I got more and more pissed, still hard as a rock and in desperate need. I found a spot on the towel that wasn't too uncomfortable, and was just starting to rut in earnest when I heard the door and voices in the main room. Walter's voice. I'd apparently slept right through Emily's visit, and now Walter had arrived for our morning shower and bandage change.

I swore a loud, hearty *motherfucker* and let the towel drop to the floor. I scooted my gym shorts back up against the bathroom wall, having to work it over my woodie. Whatever. I didn't care. My T-shirt was long enough to mostly cover it. I used the back of one bandaged hand and my knee to turn the bathroom doorknob and stomped out.

Walter and Jake were in the living room, talking. Walter gave me a nod, though he didn't smile or say hello. He'd probably heard me cursing. I glared at the two of them and went into the kitchen.

Emily had left me a large coffee travel mug on the counter with a straw in it. I took a sip. It was cold. I *thunk*ed my head against the fridge, breathing hard.

I was *so done*. Normally, I could laugh about it or take it as a challenge, but not this morning. I was frustrated and horny and resentful.

"Andy?" Jake came up behind me, his voice quiet. I heard the sink in the bathroom turn on. Walter was in there setting up for our showers. As if I'd let him near me with this fucking hard-on.

I growled, not lifting my head from the fridge. "What do you want, Jake?"

"What's the matter?"

I heard the worry in Jake's voice. He honestly didn't know? "My coffee is cold, my dick is hard, and I want to punch something. Any more questions?"

There was a smirk in Jake's voice. "So your coffee is frigid and your dick is rigid? I hate when that happens."

I smiled despite myself, though with my head on the fridge, I didn't think he could see it. But at the same time, part of me wanted to tell him to fuck off. The way he'd told me to. But I didn't. Jake wasn't doing anything wrong. He had every right to say no to my little plan. In fact, he was probably smart to say no. I was the fucked-up one. Why did I want this so much?

I sighed and slumped even more against the fridge, feeling defeated.

Behind me, I actually heard a gulp as Jake swallowed. "Hey, listen . . . I'll do it." His voice was low and gravelly, as if he didn't want Walter to hear.

I stood there, not saying anything. But my heart started pounding harder. Did he mean it?

"You said no," I finally managed. "If you don't want to do it, you shouldn't."

"I just said I would."

"Maybe now *I* don't want to," I argued, some gremlin inside me still hurt that he'd said no in the first place.

"Don't be such an emo!" Jake huffed. "Like you said, it's an expedient way to get off. It's not a big deal."

Oh thank God. My woodie had finally been starting to go down, but now it perked up again at the idea of getting some action. A warm mouth. *Jake's mouth.* Oh God. "Okay," I said breathlessly. "When?"

Jake snorted. "Eager much? We'll have to wait until Walter leaves, obviously."

That soon? Oh God. "Okay. After Walter leaves."

"Want me to ask him to nuke your coffee before I get in the shower?"

"Yeah. That'd be great. Thanks."

Jake walked away.

How did he manage to sound so cool about it? What had changed his mind?

Holy shit. Jake and I had just agreed to get naked together and suck each other off.

October 2011 - Eleventh Grade
Jake

"Dare me to do it," Andy slurred, waving around his Solo cup.

I narrowed my eyes and looked him up and down, as if considering it. I shook my head. "Nah, bro. You're drunk. You don't wanna be doing that right now."

"I'm fine!" Andy took a wobbly stumble toward me. "I have the skateboard in m'car. Dare me!"

There was a middle school football game in progress across the parking lot, but no one in our group was paying attention to it. We were all hanging out and drinking until the real Friday-night parties began. It was already dark, being around 7 p.m. in October, which made our drinking less obvious. Not that any teachers were around to see it.

My girlfriend, Denise, hugged my arm. She didn't look happy. "No way, Andy. It's a totally stupid idea to skateboard off the roof of the school, even if it were daytime, even if you weren't drunk! That's whacked."

"Yeah," I agreed, kissing her cheek. "Forget it. Just chill out and have fun."

"No! I can do it! I bet anyone thirty bucks I can. Anyone?" Andy spun in a slow circle, pointing to our friends. "Ray? Nate? Thirty bucks. Come on."

Ray shrugged. Nate and a couple of other guys shook their heads.

"No betting! No one bets. He'll break a leg. Or his neck." I spoke lazily, like I didn't really think he'd do it. I pretended to be focused on Denise. It wasn't a hardship. She was a cutie, five foot three, dark hair and eyes, and a sassy mouth. I liked her.

"Nope, I'm doing it. I'll show you." Andy put down his red Solo cup, supposedly filled with the concoction of orange juice, grapefruit juice, and rum he'd been mixing up out of his trunk. He moved around to the passenger seat of his 2009 Beamer, weaving left and right, and opened the back door.

"He's so trashed!" Nate laughed.

"Guys, don't let him do something stupid," a girl named Jayden said worriedly.

Andy dragged his skateboard out of his car, staggering slightly. *Don't overdo it*, I thought.

Andy clutched the skateboard under one arm and waved his hand. He spoke loudly, motioning to other people hanging out in the parking lot to come over. "I, Andy Tyler, am going to skateboard from the roof of this building." He waved a hand at the school. "From that point right there, near the stovepipe, or whatever that black thing is, back to here."

People began coming over. Even a few people at the football field began walking toward us.

Andy waved at me. "Jake, my man, dare me to do it. Come on!"

I pulled away from Denise and walked over to Andy. "All right. If you want to make a spectacle of yourself, I dare you. Skateboard down here from the roof, Andy. Let's see you do it!"

"He's drunk, Jake!" Denise sounded appalled.

"He won't do it!" I said dismissively. I pushed Andy a bit on his shoulder, and he did a little wobble but stayed upright. "Anyway, he's not that drunk."

"'M not that drunk!" he agreed unconvincingly. "And I'm boss on a skateboard. Been skating for, like, months!"

I bit back a laugh. Andy had been skateboarding pretty much since he could walk. Our close friends knew that, of course, but most of the gathering crowd didn't. He made some half-assed moves on the board in the parking lot, purposefully making himself look bad. The tension was building.

Nate was taking bets and people were getting upset and worried. Some were hooting at Andy to go for it, but most of the audience was trying to talk him out of it, a few getting emotional.

Gotcha.

Finally, Andy bowed and announced that he was ready to start. "Jake, if you'll be master of ceremonies."

"Sure." I pushed off the car and away from Denise. I turned to address the crowd. "Ladies and gentlemen, do not try this at home, please! They say God protects fools and drunkards, so please send up a Hail Mary for our own Andy Tyler!" I raised my hands and clapped, encouraging everyone to applaud, but most people were too freaked-out to put their hands together.

"This way, sir." I turned to Andy and swept my hand toward the building.

He started walking over there with me at his side.

"Jesus Christ, you better not really be drunk," I muttered to him when we were far enough away from the spectators.

"Nope. My cup just had juice. I'm good."

"Be careful on that drop down to the second story."

"I've got this."

"Yeah, but you've never done it in the dark." I really was worried, and it came out in my voice. "You don't have to go through with this, you know. I can pretend that I decided to call it off."

"It's fine, bro. Chill." He snuck a glance back at the crowd and chuckled. "Fuck, they are shitting their pants."

"Do *not* screw this up. If we have to call an ambulance, I'm never speaking to you again," I said darkly.

Despite the practice runs he'd made, I was still paranoid. The sprawling school consisted of a main building that was old and brick with a peaked roof over a flatter, tar-papered section. Around the main rectangle were lower additions of one and two stories. There were lots of sloped concrete struts between the levels that Andy used to drop from roof to roof. There were a few sections that were tricky, and lots of ledges had deadly drops. It could all go wrong in a heartbeat. No matter how much you planned or practiced, some things were just inherently dangerous. But Andy was an adrenaline junkie, and when he got in a certain mood, there was no talking him out of things.

Plus, I had to admit, he was really good on that damned skateboard.

We reached the double doors that led into the back hall and the locker rooms. It was unlocked thanks to the football game. Andy would go inside and make his way up various stairwells to the topmost roof, and I'd stay out here and man the video camera—and the crowd. That was the plan. But when we got to the doors, he stopped and turned to me.

"Jake."

"Yeah?"

There was a big spotlight over the doors, and he looked pale, his pupils large and black with barely a sliver of ice blue left in his eyes. "Keep your eyes on me. Okay?"

"Um . . . where else would they be?"

"No, I mean it. On *me*."

"Sure."

He studied my face for a moment, his expression intent. "You're with me. Right? It's you and me."

"You know it." I looked back toward the cars and Denise, feeling uneasy. If only Andy knew how much my eyes were on him—too often and for the wrong reasons. He'd probably hate me if he knew. But I was dating Denise now, and I was finally starting to get my head on straight.

Andy grabbed my shoulder with his free hand and shook me once. "Say it. Say it's you and me."

I looked at his face, my mouth dry. "It's you and me, Andy. Christ." I wished it were true, wished he meant it the way I wanted it to be.

"Okay." He sounded a little nervous. He dropped his hand. "Let's do this. Make sure you get good video, especially that drop by the art class window."

"I'm on it." I pulled out my phone so I could record.

"And keep talking about how drunk I am."

"Yup. I know what to do. Don't worry."

Andy grimaced. "Sorry. I know you've got this. You're the best, Jake."

Andy turned to wave in an over-the-top sloppy style to the crowd in the parking lot. Then he winked at me and went inside with his skateboard.

My stomach was in my throat for the next ten minutes as he swooped and dropped and wove, sometimes on two wheels. But he survived without a scratch. Nate made three hundred dollars that night. And my video, called "Drunken skateboard parkour," got over a hundred thousand hits on YouTube.

It would be a long time before Dunsbar High forgot the Andy and Jake Show.

Chapter
NINE

June 2017
Jake

I mentally went over my components class final exam while I took off my clothes to get into the shower. It would be humiliating to be hard in front of Walter.

As he always did, Walter adjusted the temperature of the water until he was satisfied. Then he turned back to me. I'd managed to get out of my shorts thanks to Andy's patented "wall wriggle" maneuver. I held up my hands, and Walter put plastic bags over them, sealing them with rubber bands at my wrists. Then he took my elbow and helped me step into the shower. He drew the curtain behind me to allow me time to get wet and relax for a moment under the water.

So here was one thing I could have lived my whole life without experiencing: letting an older guy like Walter bathe me. It was surprising what you could put up with when you had no choice.

"You ready?" he asked me through the curtain.

I looked down. The exam questions on semaphores had done the trick. "Yeah."

Walter pulled the curtain aside and picked up the bottle of bodywash. He was good at this—efficient, fast, and thorough. Somehow he managed to make it impersonal, maybe because he never looked me in the face. He put bodywash on his hands, then rubbed briskly over my arms and chest, doing my pits too. When he got to my junk, he was a little *too* efficient. He only did one loose pass over them and then moved on to my legs.

Was I clean enough? God, I was about to have Andy's face down there.

No. God, no, don't think about that right now.

"Can you, um, make sure I'm really clean in the, uh, groin area?" My face burned.

Walter hesitated for a moment, working over one calf. He grunted an acknowledgment. When he finished my legs, he put more soap in his hands and did another pass of the groin area, getting back between my balls with a brisk, clinical touch, getting everything super soapy.

"That good?" he asked, standing up.

"Yeah. Thanks."

He drew the curtain back, leaving me alone with my embarrassment to rinse off.

Jesus, I had agreed to do it. I'd been warring with myself for two days now, and at this point, I was sick of thinking about it. I had battling factions in my brain. One side was like, *Hey, this is your only chance to get naked with Andy, to get up close and personal with his dick, to get off together. Of course you should do it!* And the other faction was all, *You do this and you'll never get over him! You'll die of a broken heart at age forty surrounded by Star Trek memorabilia and cats!*

Left to my own devices, I probably would have opted for the safe choice—not to do it. But, as usual when Andy was in the picture, sanity went flying out the window like a teenager's boyfriend when her parents came home. He hadn't brought it up again, but I could tell he was unhappy that I'd turned it down—even hurt. For the past few days, he'd been getting more and more grumpy and irritable with horny frustration. Then this morning he'd looked so desperate, I couldn't hold out.

Well, I *could.* I didn't want to. Besides, I was in nearly as bad a shape as he was. I hadn't figured out a way to get off either.

We were doing this.

I got out of the shower before my thoughts could lead to another stray erection. Walter rubbed me down quickly with a towel and held out a pair of clean gym shorts. I stepped into them and he pulled them up. He didn't say a word until I was decent.

"You expecting company today?" he asked me as he took a comb to my hair.

"No."

"Oh. I thought maybe your girlfriend was coming to visit." His words were casual. Just something to say. Because I'd asked him for an extra-special wash of the pubes? I said nothing.

After my hair was more or less in place, he put some toothpaste on my electric toothbrush and held it up for me. I moved around on it to get all my teeth and tried not to think about other things I could impale myself on.

There was a prickling at the base of my spine and butterflies in my stomach. Were we really going to do this? It felt unreal. It wouldn't have felt any stranger if I were expecting Santa Claus and the Easter Bunny to show up for lunch. With dildos.

If Andy and I did this, I had two goals for myself: to enjoy the hell out of it physically, and to not get emotionally involved. Andy only saw it as a way to get off. I could hold on to that. I could hold on to it and not let my emotions get all tangled up in Andy again. Couldn't I?

Walter pulled the toothbrush away and filled up a small glass at the sink. He held it up to me, and I took a sip, washed it around my mouth, and spit in the sink. I turned and wiped my mouth on the towel on the rack.

Next, Walter took the plastic bags off my hands and had me sit on the toilet while he took off the bandages and swabbed my hands. They looked about the same today, red and angry, and Walter's ministrations hurt, despite his care and the numbing effect of the cream. But the pain was welcome for once. It cut through the dreamy fog in my head and made me focus on something real and mundane.

"Anything else I can do for you?" Walter asked me when I was all clean and rewrapped.

"No, I'm good." I looked at the bathroom door, feeling claustrophobic. Thankfully, Walter got the message and opened it. A blast of cool air struck my face, and I sighed with relief. I could be alone for a few minutes to gather my nerve.

"I'm ready for you, Andy!" Walter called out.

I hurried down the hall to the guest room so I didn't have to meet Andy's eyes.

Andy

I drank my coffee and ate some French toast sticks Emily had left, using the forearm tool from med supply. I felt more nervous with each passing minute, and that had helped my erection vanish, which was a good thing for now.

Walter called out that it was my turn in the shower, and I caught sight of a very clean Jake wearing only shorts going into his room. I took my shower, making myself think about anything *but* Jake while Walter was soaping me. Somehow, I got through the whole routine without embarrassing myself.

Finally, Walter left, and the cabin went into that magic lull of calm it got when the morning rush was over. The silence felt like it weighed a million pounds. I forced myself to watch out the window as Walter drove off in his little Subaru. I didn't want any chance we'd be interrupted. Once he was really gone, I raced toward the guest bedroom where Jake was staying.

The door to the room was open. I skidded to a halt in the doorway. Jake was sitting on his bed, elbows on his knees, the Kindle propped up on the nightstand.

"Hey," he said, not meeting my eyes.

He seemed nervous too. Did he seem nervous? I wasn't sure, didn't care. "Wanna do it now?" I asked quickly.

He laughed. "Impatient much?"

"Hell yeah! I'm about to burst. Aren't you?"

His grin faded into seriousness, and his Adam's apple bobbed up and down. "Pretty much, yeah."

"Okay. So is this going to be weird? It's weird, right? I don't care. How do you want to do it? Here, or my room, or what?"

I was being purposefully overeager and wide-eyed, just putting it all out there. It appeared to work. Jake's tensed body relaxed. It was just *us*, after all. No matter what we were doing, it was always just us. We could do this.

He wrinkled his nose. "Your room smells like socks and meatball subs."

"It does not," I lied.

"Here is fine." He moved over to make room for me, using his elbows to shift his body weight.

I started to get onto the bed, then changed my mind. I went to the wall and worked my ass against it to pull my gym shorts down. "Get naked," I told Jake.

He dropped his eyes, like he didn't want to see me unwrapped, as it were. I caught a glimpse of red blotchy skin at this throat. But he scooted his butt on the bed to get his waistband down, and worked his shorts off his legs.

I dove for the mattress, my dick hard and bobbing as I moved. It was weird to be in front of Jake like this, erect and blatantly out there. But the ache was back, itchier, hotter, and more insistent than ever. It was like my body knew I was about to get off and nothing was going to hold it back. And then there was Jake, sitting on the bed naked. His knees were up so I couldn't see his dick. But his eyes were locked on my erection as I got onto the bed. *I'm about to have sex with Jake.* The idea was terrifying and also thrilling, the thrill of a really good dare. And, hell, it wasn't like I'd ever been shy a day in my life.

I sat down, thought for a second, then swung on my hip so my head was toward the foot of the bed and I was staring at Jake's drawn-up thigh. "We don't have to talk about this, do we?" I teased. "Because I could really do without an Oprah moment."

Jake huffed a tiny laugh. "No. We don't have to talk about it."

"Good. Then shift over here and let's do this. Don't poke my eye out."

He huffed again but moved. And then, oh holy hell, then. Jake lay on his side, lowered his legs, and there was his dick. I had been hoping it wouldn't be entirely soft. That would have been discouraging, like he really wasn't into this, and also embarrassing given how hard I was. But he had a full-blown hard-on. It looked thick and heavy and bigger than I would have guessed from having seen him flaccid. It was a bit of a shock to be looking at another guy's tumescent prick, but not exactly a turnoff. In fact, it made that adrenaline junkie pulse twinge in my belly, like I was doing something crazy.

Then his lips closed around my head—his mouth improbably hot, the suction strong and *so good*—and I couldn't stop the whimper that came out of my mouth. I had to do something before I started groaning like a chick in a porno, so I scooted closer and tilted my head to get him inside. At first I just wanted to plug up my mouth to stop the noises. But his hips jerked in surprise, and he made a low moaning growl and pushed a little deeper, like he couldn't help it, and *holy shit*. Lust hit me hard, that slick, burning rush lighting up my body from the inside out—bam! Then logic hit me from the other side—bam! I was going down on Jake. *I'm sucking a guy's dick.* The thought threatened to kill all the good feelings with nerves and uncertainty.

I shoved the weirdness of it away, though. I was too much in need to stop this now, to let it be ruined. I tentatively moved up and down. He tasted, smelled, the way my hands smelled after I'd jerked off. There was so much of him to take in, it felt like I was choking, and I felt a flash of sympathy for the girls who'd given me head. I closed my eyes and paused, waiting to see if this was going to gross me out. But despite being unsure if I liked the act itself, my heart was pounding. What a rush. It felt so dirty, and so wrong, like I would shock people by doing it. At the very least, I shocked myself.

I breathed through my nose. It was just a penis, after all, and I'd pulled my own often enough. I stopped moving my head and instead just sucked him like a hard candy, trying to get used to it, rolling him in my mouth as much as space and his rigidity would allow. I could feel the shape of his head against the roof of my mouth. The skin along his shaft was softer than anything I'd ever felt on my tongue, but it covered firm flesh. It was . . . sexy. Base. Raw. I rubbed the flat of my tongue up and down over the rim of his head the way I liked and . . . as if echoing me, Jake stopped what he was doing and did that to me too. He held me in his mouth, sucked lightly, and rubbed my ridge hard with the flat of his tongue.

Oh gods above. That felt incredible. Lust washed through me again, fast and fierce, and suddenly my nerves vanished. The flesh in my mouth was exactly what I wanted. I liked being filled, gagged. I liked the way Jake trembled, like I was driving him crazy. And it was *Jake*. I'd thought about this before, but never expected to *actually* do it. My balls tightened and tingles shot up my spine.

God, I was so damn horny. I wanted to thrust, but I didn't, because if I did, it would be over too soon. I stayed still so we could keep doing this, teasing each other with tongues and suction, letting pleasure coil through me like thick, hot molasses. And it was trippy too. With us both doing the same thing, and my eyes closed, I almost *could* imagine I was doing it to myself, that the hard dick in my mouth was my own. That Jake and I were one person.

I pulled off long enough to breathe a curse. "Fucking hell."

"Yeah. 'S good," Jake panted in agreement before going back at it.

This time, when I took him in my mouth, it was because I wanted it, was hungry for it. Some of that was pure physical lust because of the way he was sucking me. But I *did* want it. Him. I wanted Jake. I wanted him to say *it's good* again. I wanted to hear that needy wobble in his voice. I wanted to make him feel as fantastic as he was making me feel. I wanted to make him come. I wanted to be the one with him—not fucking *Kevin*.

I hooked a forearm over his hip so I could hold him steady, and took him in deeper, started moving him in and out. I liked it better when I moved his hip with my forearm instead of bobbing my head. That felt dirtier somehow, like he was fucking my mouth and I had to take it. Jake groaned and sort of attacked me, an all-out assault, sucking and licking and bobbing. He thrust into my mouth more forcefully, erratically.

Oh God. God. Okay. Shit. I was going to come. It had been too long, and this was too real and new and exciting. I closed my eyes and let myself go with it, drown in it. Jake thrust into my mouth, overwhelming my senses, silencing me, stealing my breath. On the other end, he was giving me the best blowjob of my life, the suction and pace so good I couldn't hold back. His tongue drove me wild. His entire body trembled.

I made a choked sound around his dick as my balls tightened unbearably and I started to pulse. I tried to move my hips back, but his forearm clung to me fiercely. He gave a garbled groan, and I felt a burst of sour taste in my mouth. Right. Fuck. I should have thought about this moment ahead of time, planned for it. But I hadn't. I would have pulled off and finished him with my hand, except I had no hand and I wasn't going to leave him hanging in space with no friction.

So I stayed put, swallowing quickly and trying not to gag. It wasn't pleasant, but since I was still riding the aftershocks of my own orgasm, I couldn't be too arsed about it.

When it was all over, I fell away from him bonelessly. I lay on my back, waiting for my heart to stop trying to escape from my chest. I wiped my face with the crook of my arm.

"Man, that was gay," I joked.

From somewhere near my feet, Jake started to laugh in a low rumble. "Ya think?"

Then I laughed, and we were lost in hysterical giggles. It felt good—release of a tension of a different kind. And it meant Jake and I were all right.

Jake punched my leg lightly with his elbow. "It was your idea, bro."

"Yeah. And it was brilliant, if I do say so myself," I said casually. "It did the trick, right?"

"I can hardly deny it."

That made me feel a little smug. "So you cool with doing this again? Till we get our hands back?"

"Jesus, we just finished. Give me ten minutes," Jake joked.

"I don't mean *now*."

"Yeah, all right." Jake's voice was a little gruff. I ignored it.

"Cool." I rolled off the bed and looked for my shorts, only to see them crumpled up on the floor. I sighed, and made a show of it— wiggled my toes into the leg holes, maneuvered my feet and calves around trying to work the shorts up to my knees, and then used the wall to work them the rest of the way up over my ass. I used the tip of my bandaged hand to flip the elastic waistband over my junk. I waggled my eyebrows at Jake as I did it.

By the time I was done, Jake was grinning like a jackal, the worry gone from his face.

Mission accomplished.

Chapter
TEN

Jake

A ndy and I had had sex. That was a thing that had happened. Fortunately, Andy seemed perfectly normal afterward, even being intentionally goofy. It dispelled the awkward immediately.

Postorgasm, we went out to sit in the sun. I hadn't had much breakfast, and I had the postsex munchies. I would have loved to take a bag of pretzels onto the dock and snack, but eating was such a hassle that I dismissed the idea. Emily had made us wraps, as usual, and they were in the fridge, but I'd eat that later when I was starving enough that it was worth all the effort and mess.

"Want to watch some of *Walking Dead* tonight?" Andy asked as we got settled into the warmth and the lassitude.

"If you want. Or *Plan Z* is on the Syfy channel tonight," I suggested.

"What's that?"

"It's a zombie movie. *Plan Z-eeeeee.*" I drew out the letter ominously.

He shuddered. "I dunno. My dad talks about 'plan Z.' Not really good associations for me."

"Oh? What's your dad's 'plan Z'?" Knowing Andy's dad, it was probably some stock scheme.

Andy put his feet up on the little wooden table we used as a foot bench. The sight of his long, bare legs, dusted with blond hair, did weird things to my gut. "My dad had a client, for like fifteen years.

And this guy kept doing things to secure a good retirement. First he worked for a start-up company. Bio-tech or something. He gave ten years of his life to it. It was supposed to go public and make him all this money because he had tons of stock."

"Yeah."

"Only then it went wrong, some patents fell through or something, and the company went bankrupt."

"That sucks."

"Right. So then this guy started his own business, invested his savings, sure he was going to earn a few million to fund his retirement. But the business never took off."

I had a feeling this story didn't have a happy ending.

"So then he wrote a book, tried to make it a blockbuster, was going to get a movie deal and all that. Only the book came out and sold a hundred copies or something. There were some other things too I don't remember. But the guy kept saying this is 'plan B' then 'plan C' and so on."

"So what happened?" It was almost like telling ghost stories. I settled in my chair, appreciating the rays of the sun and the sound of the water lapping the shore. I propped my feet up on the bench too.

"Finally, this guy hits his sixtieth birthday, and he had no retirement and not much savings left. He hadn't paid off his mortgage because he was always investing in these schemes. He joked to my dad that 'plan X' was that he was going to keep working for the rest of his life."

"Bummer."

"Only then he got sick and couldn't work."

Andy stopped as if that were the end of the story.

"So what was 'plan Z'?" I prompted.

Andy put two fingers in his mouth and pulled the trigger.

"Oh my God!" I said, disgusted and horrified. It was one thing to tell ghost stories, but this was too real and not funny at all.

Andy shrugged. "I know. But it happens. It happens more than you'd think. My dad sees it all the time." His voice sounded strained.

"Well, Christ, Andy. You're not going to end up with plan Z!"

"I know I'm not," Andy said firmly. "Because I won't let that happen. But like my dad said, nothing's guaranteed. Even if you work hard, you might not get there. Top law firms like the one my mom works for, they have good retirement bennies and golden parachutes and stuff like that. Very few companies have that anymore. Does Neverware have a pension plan?"

I mentally reviewed my employment contract. "No. But they have a 401K."

Andy nodded, as if he'd expected as much. "You need to max that out, Jake, every single year. Don't wait."

"Jesus, I'm twenty-two, bro! I need to get an apartment and a car and other stuff to just *live* first."

"Don't put it off, man. I'm telling you," Andy said gravely.

I rolled my eyes behind my sunglasses. Andy's dad had sure done a number on him. Not that it was a *bad* thing, being concerned about your future. Andy was lucky to have a dad who gave a shit, tried to teach him things. That was way better than my dad. And it was all smart, I knew that. But I wanted to at least live a little before I started worrying about my retirement. I didn't say it.

"So this is your agenda?" I asked. "Seduce my nubile self and then terrify me?"

Andy snorted. "Sorry. I don't know why that even came up." He leaned forward and took a drink of his iced tea.

"Gah! Depressing. Maybe we should discuss the Holocaust while we're at it. Or leprosy."

He nudged my leg with his foot. We'd taken to doing that, using our feet to express things our hands couldn't right now. But, this time, his foot lingered, trailing down my calf and then settling half over mine, the cool of his bare sole on the sun-heated top of my foot. I swallowed.

"We could watch *Vikings*," I suggested. "We have it queued up on Netflix."

"Yeah, let's. I've been dying to get to that."

We sat on the dock, and Andy chatted away about Vikings—the real-life ones, which he'd read a couple of history books about. But my mind began to roam elsewhere.

Looking at his long, sturdy foot so casually draped over mine, I got a warm, nervous, swoopy feeling in my stomach, something like

I imagined astronauts would feel in zero gravity. My mind went back to what had happened less than an hour ago,

I had sex with Andy. I'd seen him hard. I'd had him in my mouth. I'd swallowed his come. And he had done the same to me. Talk about a mind-fuck. I'd spent *years* fantasizing about that, and it had just happened.

It had been awkward at first. When I'd imagined getting naked with Andy, it hadn't been like that. I'd imagined kissing and other stuff first, easing into it. But what we'd done was just—*Hey, here's my stiffy, let's get off.* It'd been weird because there was a strain of us-ness to it that was so casual and everyday. Like we were hanging out doing any old thing. Like we were just two bros jerking off.

At first. But then he was right in front of me, hard and perfect and *real.* So undeniably real. The moment he pushed into my mouth, the awkward was wiped away. I felt a lust so massive and powerful it was like an avalanche that had been building up and building up, held in place by the thinnest spider's web. That web had snapped, *ka-pow!*

God, the sensation of him in my mouth, the excitement of being that close to him, smelling him, tasting him, getting him off; the incredible hotness of being up close and personal with his hard dick, his inexperienced enthusiasm on the other side. I loved the way he'd just gone for it, the way he did everything else—wholeheartedly and with determination. And he *had* liked it. Sure, he'd been horny as fuck and probably could have gotten off in a stiff breeze. But still. It hadn't put him off. The gay thing. The cock-in-his-mouth thing. He hadn't gone soft, and he'd moaned around my—

Oh God, I was getting boned up again sitting on the dock.

"So. Vikings." I cleared my throat.

"Huh?"

I'd interrupted some monologue Andy had been giving about longships.

I scrambled for something more intelligent to say. "Um . . . those were the same ships used to invade France too? Because they're long and . . . ships?"

There was a moment of silence, then Andy laughed as if I'd said the funniest thing. "You weren't listening, were you? I've been prattling on for ten minutes!"

"I was making an effort to be polite," I said, faking a hurt tone.

"Yeah, well, fail." Andy nudged his sunglasses onto his forehead with his wrist and looked at my crotch. "Already? God, Jake. You're incorrigible."

His foot had moved off mine at some point, so I kicked him lightly in the leg. "I'm just sitting here! I'm innocent as a baby."

"No, I was just sitting here talking, authentically, about important historical facts, and you're over there with a glazed look thinking about sex."

"I am not!" I lied.

He chuckled. "I wonder if we could manage to last longer than two minutes this time? What do you think?" His tone was both flirty and utterly natural. And there was a dare in there too. I forgot how to breathe.

"Ten minutes," I suggested, when I could speak again. "We could have Siri set a timer. No coming till it goes off."

"You're on. But if one person says 'stop,' the other person has to pause."

"Agreed."

I wasn't sure which of us moved first, but in under sixty seconds we were back on my bed, naked.

Siri held our balls to the fire, but we both outlasted her.

Dare #3

ELEVEN

NOVEMBER 2012 - TWELFTH GRADE
ANDY

I t was a Saturday in November. We still had a week before Thanksgiving break, but the skies were clear, the ground was snow-free, and the air was not so cold that it shriveled your balls. I suggested we all meet at the quarry to hang out. It would probably be our last chance to be outside before winter bitch-slapped Boston hard.

Jake had broken up with Denise, and I was only sometimes seeing a girl who lived in DC, so we rode to the quarry together in my Beamer, complete with a bag of deli sandwiches, a case of beer hiding under a blanket in the trunk, and my dirt bike mounted on the back. Word had spread, as I'd hoped it would, and when we got to the quarry, there were about twenty kids from Dunsbar already there.

Quincy Quarries was an awesome hangout place. It was all rocks and water and thick greenery trying to overgrow everything, but you could see the skyline of downtown Boston in the distance, so it still felt urban. During the summer, there were rock climbers and people swimming, but it was too cold for that in November.

Jagged rocky walls surrounded the abandoned quarry pit, which was filled with murky water. Many of the stones were garish with graffiti. At the top of the tallest cliff were a couple of iron pins. If you were daring, and fairly stupid, you could jump off at that spot into the water below. But I'd done that plenty of times, and so had Jake. I was looking for a much bigger challenge.

There was a stack of forms and brochures on my desk at home, letters of acceptance, and deadlines looming down on me. I was dialed up to eleven with tension and I needed . . . I needed the Andy and Jake Show.

We sat around on a bunch of rocks, sharing the food people had brought and drinking beer. I nursed a single bottle, making it last, and I noticed Jake fake-drinking his. I caught him looking at me a dozen times, a question in his eyes. He wiped his hands on his jeans more than usual. Jake was nervous. Me too, only my blood thrummed. I felt alive, almost sick with anticipation. Finally I stood up.

"I brought my dirt bike. Anyone who wants to try it can." I went to unload the bike, and Jake, Nate, and a couple of other guys went with me.

We rode around the dirt area next to the quarry for a bit. I let five guys and two girls who wanted to try it take a turn. I wasn't weird about my stuff. It was just a dirt bike. My dad would probably go ballistic if he saw this, though more out of fear of liability than worry about the cost of the bike. Fortunately, no one wiped out or hurt themselves.

And finally it was time.

"So who thinks I can jump the quarry on this bike?" I called out.

Some of them had been there for the drunken rooftop parkour, and all of them had at least heard about it. Some of the guys, like Nate, began to whoop.

"Yeah, do it, Andy!"

"All right! Let's see this!"

"Go for it!"

But of course there were a lot of people arguing that it couldn't, or shouldn't, be done.

Well, it *couldn't* be done, not in most places. The quarry was really wide, like hundreds of feet. Everyone trailed after us as Jake and I walked around. We pretended we were scouting out a good spot.

The spot I'd previously picked out was where a channel of water cut through the rocks. Two cliffs were divided by about fifty feet, and one cliff was a good five feet below the other. Neither the vertical nor the horizontal jumps were all that spectacular. I'd seen guys online do jumps seventy, eighty, even ninety feet wide on bikes in a lower class than my 450 Yamaha. But it sure as shit looked dramatic with the ragged rock walls and a long drop to the rocks and trickle of water below. If you fucked it up, you'd be carried out in a body bag.

"There." I pointed up at the higher cliff. "I'll jump across *that.*"

"I don't know, Andy." Jake looked up at the cliff with a worried expression. "Let's look for something else. That's gotta be eighty feet across, and no one's ever jumped more than seventy feet on a dirt bike."

Rule number one of a good stunt: make it *seem* way more dangerous than it actually was. You needed to make the crowd believe no one had ever done what you were about to attempt, or they'd died doing it. Frame of reference, perception, was eighty percent of all tricks. I doubted anyone here would challenge Jake's statements—and they didn't.

The usual protests, concerns, and warnings began. People didn't want me to do it. I was going to kill myself! Nate started taking bets. He wasn't even in on the plan; he just liked to bet.

I never took any money for my stunts. That wasn't the point. I wasn't doing it to fleece people. And Jake didn't bet either. But if Nate wanted to do his wheeling and dealing, that was on him. It had the added benefit of making the onlookers even more invested.

"Dare me, Jake?" I asked him, holding out my hand for a wrist grab.

He eyed me thoughtfully. "Nah, man. Not this time. If you're doing that jump, I'm going with you."

"What? No way!" I looked him up and down. "You weigh what, one forty? You'll totally throw off the bike. I'll be lucky to make the jump as it is."

"Don't care. If you want to kill yourself, you'll have to take me with you this time." Jake folded his arms and glared at me, clearly prepared to not back down.

Ten minutes later, Jake was on the back of my Yamaha, arms locked around my waist. At least a dozen people stood around filming us on their phones, and a half dozen more looked up at us from the bottom of the cliff. A couple of girls were crying. The crowd grew strangely somber.

The atmosphere was tense with dread, the air eerily quiet as we sat in position on the bike, well back from the jump. Two crows started up and flew across my view. Boston was visible but not audible, and the November air was still and cold as the grave.

It was like a bad omen or something. If I'd been Catholic, I would have crossed my chest. Jake and I had practiced a similar jump at the motocross park. I knew we could make it, technically. But being over a ravine caused a fear to ignite in my belly that I hadn't anticipated.

It wasn't myself I was scared for, I realized, but Jake. He'd insisted on doing this with me, said he was tired of me getting all the glory. And it was way more dramatic with two on the bike. But now that I was there at the starting line with his warm weight pressed behind me, I had a stark awareness of how alive he was. How fragile.

I turned my head over my shoulder to look at him, hoped he could hear me despite his helmet. "You sure?" I whispered. "Not too late to back out."

His brown eyes looked a little frightened, but he shook his head and squeezed me tighter. "If you go, I go." His voice was a tether that snaked around me and held.

And I felt relief. I nodded, turned back around, patted his hand in warning, and started the bike. The sound of the motor was a loud roar in the thin air. I mentally went through a checklist, but time felt slippery. It might have been five seconds or five minutes before I released the clutch and we peeled out across the top of the cliff. *Closer. Closer.* Jake about cut me in half he held me so tight, and yet it wasn't tight enough. Someone screamed, maybe it was me, and then we were flying.

There was only air, the wind whipping me, sheer terror-joy, and a breathless moment of defying gravity before it pulled us down.

We landed, jolting so hard both Jake and I would have bruises for a week where his chin guard hit me between my shoulders. I managed to keep the bike upright, and the moment we stopped, Jake hopped off. I slammed down the kickstand and got off too, whooping and jumping around, overflowing with an incredible high. Jake grabbed me and we hugged, survivors, daredevils.

I never wanted him to let go.

June 2017
Jake

For the next few weeks, Andy and I had a ton of sex. We were getting off three times a day. After all, we had little else to do, it was fun, it didn't require hands, and helped us forget the pain and discomfort of our burns for a short while. Andy was almost always the instigator.

"I had no idea you were such a horndog," I told him after the third day. We were lying in bed after round three, head to foot and staring at the ceiling. "Maybe you should get that checked."

"I'm a red-blooded male, what can I say?"

"Purple-blooded maybe. Or you're being dosed. What's the opposite of that saltpeter shit they give inmates in prison? Viagra, let's just go with that. Maybe the township here puts it in the water."

"Apparently. Because *you've* been keeping up with me just fine, Jakey," Andy pointed out dryly.

Which was true. Then again, I was sexually attracted to him like crazy, whereas I figured I was just a means to an end for him. So I was surprised he was so enthusiastic.

Despite how much we were having sex, the act itself was always the same. Sixty-nine. It would be on my bed or Andy's bed. We'd get each other off and not touch before or after or anytime in between. When we weren't sucking each other off, we were total bros. There was nothing except those two extremes.

On the last Monday in June, we were in the kitchen after lunch. It was really hot outside, the kind of humid, heavy East Coast air that was rife with mosquitoes. We weren't in a hurry to leave the comfort of the cottage's air conditioning, despite there being nothing exciting to do inside. I was bent practically double at the fridge trying to put away the mustard bottle I had gripped between my wrists. When I straightened up and turned, I caught Andy checking out my ass.

He didn't pretend he wasn't looking, either. Instead, he sort of shrugged, raised his eyebrows at me, and grinned. But the heated, flirty glint in his eyes was unmistakable. "Nice ass there, Jakey."

"Yeah, it is. Don't think you're ever gonna tap it, though," I joked to hide the blush I could feel burning my face. I glanced down at his crotch to make my meaning clear, and saw he had a semi going in his silky gym shorts.

My knees went a little wobbly. Had Andy really gotten aroused just by looking at my ass? *My* ass?

Maybe it was because we'd already sucked each other off dozens of times, including just the night before, but my normal filters were weak. As in practically nonexistent. In that moment of want, I did what I'd only fantasized about doing before. I kicked the fridge door shut with my foot, and went up to him. He was leaning against the kitchen table, a sturdy pine rectangle with four chairs. I nudged my chest against him and pushed his legs apart with my thighs. I wanted to kiss him, dear God. But I didn't dare. No, I had that much sanity left at least. That would give the game away, expose me.

His eyes went half-lidded, and he helped me as I used the tips of my bandaged hands to push at his elastic waistband. He wiggled, and I pushed, and soon his shorts were crumpled on the floor. I nudged him back until he sat on the table. Damn, I loved that table fiercely at that moment. It was just the right height to allow me to get to my knees.

It was broad daylight in the kitchen, and this was *Andy*, my best friend, but I didn't care. This was a fantasy I'd run through my mind a hundred times over the years, and I had the chance to go for it. I wasn't sure I could have stopped if I wanted to.

I nudged his legs apart with my shoulders. He was exposed, utterly and unabashedly revealed—every freckle, every hair, every fascinating wrinkle and furl, but Andy didn't seem to mind. And *oh my God*.

My face was level with the core of him—the base of his dick, as it continued to fill and rise toward his stomach; his balls, which were a bit loose and ruddy-skinned and fuzzy with dark-blond hair; and the sweet plumpness where his ass met the tabletop. He was so gorgeous. So perfect, it caused my breath to hitch. Of course, I'd seen him a lot over the past few days, but never so well lit, never so open. My throat closed up and my pulse beat in my ears. I had enough sense left, though, to try to play this off as no big deal.

I looked up at him. He was watching me, his face serious, but otherwise unreadable.

"Let me try it without you doing me at the same time. It might be easier." My voice wobbled only a little.

"Okay." He attempted a laugh, but it came out a nervous sort of titter.

Justification out of the way, I let myself go. I leaned forward and ran the flat of my tongue over one of his balls and then sucked it gently into my mouth. I closed my eyes.

This. God. It was Andy's body and Andy's flesh, his sex. Raw and so real it hurt. I pushed down a sticky glob of emotions and focused on the physical. Part of me wanted to show Andy what I could do, to tease and torture him and worship him with my mouth, to force him to remember me. Maybe someday, when he was forty years old and married and bored, he'd think of this summer and of how good it had been. But another part of me was afraid of giving myself away, of revealing how much I loved his dick or, worse, loved *him*.

But, Jesus, the heat and smell and taste of him as I sucked under his balls, rubbed hard with my tongue at his perineum, and thrust into that tantalizing crease. Andy's breathing went harsh and labored. He lay back on his elbows and lifted one foot to the tabletop, spreading himself further. I nudged the other leg up and over my shoulder.

"*Jake, Jesus,*" he gasped as I went for it, rolling over his furl with my tongue. "You're insane."

I stopped and drew back, looking up into his eyes. "*You're* telling *me* something's too risky?"

He managed a smirk. "Hell no. Keep doing it." He pressed against my shoulder with his calf, making it clear I wasn't supposed to stop.

I'd never done this before. It wasn't something Kevin and I'd ever done or that I'd even fantasized about. But I wanted to worship Andy, to drive him crazy, learn him in every way possible. I wanted to do something he'd never forget. I licked over his rim, tasting a hint of soap from his morning shower with Walter. Encouraged at the clean taste, I licked again and again, flicking the tip of my tongue sharply against his puckered skin or rubbing it hard and flat, and alternating that attention with sucking his balls and the insides of his thighs so that when I went back to his pink furl, it always made him shiver and gasp.

It was effective. Before long, Andy was squirming and moaning, thrusting slightly into the air. He pushed me down with the leg that was hooked over my shoulder, as if he could hold me where he wanted me.

"Fuck. Jake. Fuck," he repeated with hisses and whimpers.

Damn, he was really sensitive there. I longed for my fingers. I wanted nothing more than to work a finger into him as I licked and to see if I could find his prostate, see if that would make him even more wild. And that made me think about fucking him, an image even my most secret heart had never dared conjure up before. I made an animal sound and pierced him as deeply as I could with my tongue.

I was throbbing in my shorts, so hard I was ready to pull down his other leg and rut against his calf. But before I could, Andy begged me, "Jesus, please, Jake, make me come. *Please*. I can't take any more." His voice was desperate and his thighs shook.

I couldn't refuse him. I got to my feet and bent over him, taking his dick into my mouth and sucking him down hard and fast.

He gave a choked scream and tried to thrust his hips off the table. I worked him intently, in and out of my mouth, suction dragging against him on every withdrawal. He let loose a steady stream of moans, and his leg skittered like a live wire against my hip. He was close.

"Don't stop, don't stop, don't stop," he chanted.

I didn't stop. When he came, he did so with a string of curses. His body bowed, curling in over his stomach. I glanced up to see his eyes rolled back in his head with the force of it.

God, oh God, I needed to come.

If I'd had my hands, I would have been working myself already, but I didn't. Andy's foot that had been on the table flopped down as he finished spasming and collapsed on the table. I hooked my arm around it and ground against him. Working my pulsing flesh against the bone of his calf.

"Jake—" he started, dreamily, probably about to offer to return the favor.

But I panted, my cheek on his thigh. I was so close. That had been the hottest thing I'd ever experienced, getting Andy that worked up, that he'd let me, that he was so sensitive there, that I'd—

I came in my shorts, burying my groan in his lap.

And then, as my flesh shrank and the pleasure faded, my heart seized up. I couldn't raise my head. That. That hadn't been just two bros getting the job done. I'd been so turned on rimming him, at the smell and taste of him, I'd rutted against his leg *like an animal*. Shame washed through me, hot and ugly.

I realized he had to feel the burning in my cheeks, pressed as I was to his thigh. But I couldn't move. I wasn't sure I could bear to face him long enough to get up and run to my room.

Then I felt his heel run along my back. "Christ, you fucking killed me. Warn a guy next time."

His words were teasing, but his voice sounded tight. Did it sound tight? Was he embarrassed for me? *Well, duh. You think?* I swallowed.

Still, his words were enough to unfreeze me. I straightened up, not meeting his gaze. "Well . . . that was gross. Me, I mean. My shorts. Um. I'll go clean up. Wash, wash, wash your cares away. And spunk too!"

He snickered. It sounded muffled, so I dared a look at him. He had his arm over his face, as if exhausted. Which meant I didn't have to see what was on his face, thank God. And he hardly looked sophisticated, lying there with his softening junk. Maybe it wasn't so bad, what I'd done? Maybe I could play it off as just a horny-guy thing?

"You're such a dork," he teased.

"Well obviously." My voice sounded raw, just like I felt.

I left him there and escaped to the bathroom. Maybe somehow he'd missed the way I'd not only reveled in the gayest of gay sex but also pretty much admitted my feelings for him by worshipping his body and humping his leg. Maybe we could pretend it hadn't happened.

From now on, I wasn't going to initiate anything sexual, I promised myself. Not even a smoky glance. *Andy* would have to initiate if he wanted more. And then I would only do the minimum required. No more rimming. No more rutting wildly against him like his very smell got me off. Even though it did.

Dear God, how long could I hide it? It wasn't even July yet. We still had most of the summer in front of us.

Chapter
TWELVE

ANDY

We'd been at the cottage for over a month and—as scenic as the Nantucket Sound was, as great as hanging out with *Jake* was— we were both climbing the walls. It would have been way more boring without the sex. God, I'd never *had* so much sex. Blowjobs on tap, why *wouldn't* we do that three or four times a day? But even so, you could only have sex for so many of your waking hours, more's the pity. Especially since Jake was stupidly good at getting me off and seemed disinclined to drag it out lately. I'd loved it that day he'd gotten adventurous in the kitchen and *rimmed* me. God. That was so insanely hot! I would have been up for lots more exploration like that. But Jake had acted awkward afterward, and since then, we'd stuck to the efficient sixty-nine.

One morning Emily lingered over coffee. "Our place is a lot smaller than this," she said. "But we have a pontoon boat and a barbeque grill. Would you guys like to come over for dinner tonight? You must be ready for a change of pace."

"Oh my *God*, yes," Jake said at once, in a tone of joking desperation. Then he looked at me as if wondering if he'd spoken too soon.

But I nodded at him, silently agreeing. "Definitely. I think I've memorized the cracks on every ceiling of this joint."

"Yeah, this *joint*," Jake teased. "The ol' Cape Cod slammer. We've named all the spiders too. Ethel is my favorite."

I jabbed him with an elbow. *Dork.* "It's nice of you to offer, Emily. You've done a lot for us already."

"Well, I am getting paid for it." Emily raised an eyebrow. "But tonight is 'just because.'"

"That's my favorite reason," Jake said. He held up his hands. "What can we bring? We've got plenty of spare bandages and antibiotic cream."

Emily chuckled. "Yeah, that's okay. I've got it covered. Bob's boss gave him a box of steaks, so we've got meat to spare."

I studiously refused to look at Jake because I knew we'd bust out laughing if I did. *Meat to spare.* God, I was mature.

"Pick you guys up at five?" Emily offered.

"Sounds good," I said.

The house where Emily and Bob lived was tiny. It looked like it had been built fifty years ago as a summer fishing cabin and had been converted to a year-round dwelling on the cheap. It couldn't be more than a thousand square feet, and it was on a gnarly part of the coastline where there was a big drop down to the sound. The front of the cabin had a log face with white plaster between the beams and a front porch that was only about two feet wide and listed to the left, giving the impression of a crooked smile.

The inside was modest but clean. There was an open space that made up the living room, dining room, and kitchen. It had big windows that overlooked the water far down below. And there was a short hall that probably led to a bedroom and bath, probably just one of each given the size of the place. From the Formica cabinets to the old plaid couch, nothing was new or fancy, but the room felt cheerful and homey. There were braided rugs on the floor in bright colors, comfortable throws and pillows everywhere, and the fridge door was covered in stuff.

While Emily and Jake chatted about the view, I took a step closer to see what was on the fridge. It was covered with ceramic heart frames in various sizes and colors, from pink polka dots to gold glitter. Each frame contained a photo of Emily and Bob. There was a large

$B + E$ in plastic letters in the middle too. It was like a shrine to their coupledom and the sappiest thing I'd ever seen, but it gave me a pang of . . . something. Jealousy? Envy? Maybe that.

I couldn't imagine something like that at my parents' house. Dear God, no. And I couldn't imagine it with any girl I'd dated either. Amber would have called it *tacky*. She was more the ultra-modern chrome-kitchen type, with the Jag in the garage.

"Hey, guys." Bob came in the back door, a wide smile on his face.

I'd seen Bob a few times when he'd been working on our yard. He was tall, maybe six foot three, with broad shoulders, a spare tire, a lumpy but good-natured face, and floppy brown hair. He wore a navy-blue T-shirt over tan cargo shorts and had flip-flops on his big feet. He went to the fridge and pulled out a pan covered in foil.

"Hey," said Jake. "Thanks for having us over."

"Good to see you, Bob. How's it going?" I normally would have offered my hand for a shake, but since I couldn't do that, I just nodded my chin in greeting.

"Me? I'm great." Bob put the pan on the counter and took off the foil. It was filled with steaks in a brown marinade. He turned them with a fork, glancing at our hands with a slight frown. "What about you guys? Are your burns getting better?"

"Oh yeah," said Jake. "It's feels like it's going really slow, but it is getting easier. Our nurse, Walter, says that we're probably past the point where any infection is likely, or, you know, our hands falling off. So there's that."

"That's good news. I hate it when my hands fall off." Bob smirked at Jake. He went back to turning meat in the tray. "I hope you guys both like steak. 'Cause we're having steak, steak, and steak."

"Oh, we are not!" Emily scolded lightly. "I also have a pasta salad, baked beans, and chips. But I've been feeding these two for weeks. They're carnivores all right."

Jake gave me a private, raised brow look that said he was agreeing with the carnivore statement. I looked away, not wanting to think about having Jake's dick in my mouth while in polite company.

"Steak sounds great, thank you," I told Bob. "But it might not be graceful."

Emily laughed. "Don't worry. I'll cut it up for you guys. And if you can't manage the pieces with that eating tool of yours, I'll even hand-feed you. It'll be good practice." She patted her stomach.

"You're expecting?" Jake said with surprise.

"Yup. Our little girl will be here in January." Emily glowed like a winter fire. She stepped over to Bob, who kissed her appreciatively on the mouth, and not quickly either. It was as if Jake and I vanished for a moment.

Their kiss was warm and completely self-absorbed. Bob ducked his head and Emily was up on her tiptoes, like they'd had years of practice.

I looked at Jake, who was staring out the window, probably embarrassed. There was a not entirely pleasant burning sensation in my gut. It was weird. Jake and I had sucked each other off for a few weeks now, but we'd never done something as simple as kiss.

Simple? Was it? Somehow it seemed gayer than what we'd been doing. You needed attraction to really kiss someone. Oral sex, you could sort of zone out and imagine . . . whatever you wanted to imagine. Whatever got you there. But kissing—that was right in someone's face. It was even more intimate than staring into another person's eyes up close. You had to like a person to do that.

And I did. Like Jake. I wanted to kiss him, I realized. On the mouth, deep and with intent. I looked at his mouth, imagining what it would be like.

"We've been fixing up a nursery," Bob said, his arms still wrapped around Emily.

"Yeah, it's basically a large pantry. We had to remove the shelves. We call her our 'closet baby.'" Emily laughed.

"You guys won't look for a bigger place?" I asked, without thinking. It sounded impolite.

But Emily just shook her head. "Nah. I want to spend my spare time with my family, not cleaning a big house or watching Bob sweat over the lawn. I've managed enough big properties to know how much work they are. We're happy here."

"Cool." I nodded, feeling stupid for having asked.

Bob gave Emily one last kiss and moved to put the pan of steaks back in the fridge. "These should marinate a bit longer. You guys wanna go out on the pontoon boat? Emily said you aren't supposed to get in the water, but I promise it's safe. I've never had anyone go overboard yet."

"I'd love that," Jake said quickly.

"Yeah, great," I agreed. I'd been missing taking out the speedboat or, even better, the jet skis. It sucked to be at the cottage and not be able to do that.

Bob and Emily's pontoon boat was old but good-sized. It fit the four of us with room to spare. It was the sort of achingly safe family boat that I normally would have rolled my eyes at, but at this point, I was happy for any vessel someone else would drive. We cruised up and down the sound awhile, going into some quaint coves and a natural wetlands area. We chatted and drank beer.

"Do you manage a lot of properties around the sound?" Jake asked Emily.

"Eighteen different ones right now," she said. "It's a lot, but usually not all of them need me at the same time. It's my busiest season. Winters are quiet."

"She writes all winter," Bob put in with an admiring shake of his head.

"You write?" I asked, surprised.

"Yeah," Emily said in a breezy tone. "I self-pub books on Amazon. It's not a big deal really."

"What kind of books?" Jake asked. "No, let me guess . . ." He studied her thoughtfully. "Self-help titles. Maybe involving real estate or organization."

"I'm glad you think I'm together enough to write that sort of thing, but sadly, no."

"Motorcycle maintenance?" Jake teased. "I can totally see you in black leather."

She laughed. "Actually, you're not far off. I write horror."

"Seriously?" I asked.

"Oh my God, you deviant!" Jake pretended to be shocked.

I pushed his leg with my foot. He was such a dork.

"Deviant is right." Bob shuddered. "I can't even read her stuff, it's so scary. Lots of murders at waterfront cabins. It would give me nightmares!"

"Hey, write what you know!" Emily said cheerfully.

"Great. You have a serial killer delivering all our meals." Jake gave me a grimace.

"In her defense, she's a good cook," I pointed out.

"So when you say we're having steak for dinner . . ." Jake hedged.

"Tonight's menu features plain-old cow, I'm afraid. And don't worry about the meal service. I never write about poisoners. I'm more into bladed weapons."

"Well, that's a relief," Jake huffed.

"What makes you want to write horror?" I asked.

Emily shrugged, her button nose wrinkling up. "I've always been a huge horror fan. I grew up reading Stephen King and Dean Koontz, V.C. Andrews, John Saul. It's an addiction."

"We both like horror movies," Bob put in. "Though I'm more the psychological suspense type, and Emily loves slashers."

"No kidding?" Jake said. "What's the best horror movie you've seen recently?"

Emily gave it a second's thought. "*The Babadook*. Awesome movie. And probably my mommy hormones are showing."

"Nah, that's my favorite too," Bob put in. "But I can't stay in the room when she's got Eli Roth on. We'll see if those mommy hormones soften her a bit."

"Never," Emily said with conviction.

"Andy and I watch horror movies sometimes," Jake said. "But he gets all scared and grabs my arms. He's such a baby."

I rolled my eyes. "Just know that sixty percent of what comes out of Jake's mouth has no relationship to reality."

"Good." Emily smiled. "I like a man with a healthy imagination."

We chatted about horror movies for a while. Then Bob talked about his work. When he wasn't helping Emily out with property maintenance, he worked part-time managing a gift shop in Osterville.

I watched them chatter easily about their schedules, and I wondered. They seemed genuinely happy even though they obviously didn't have a ton of money. Money wasn't everything, I knew that. But it was a lot. It was peace of mind, as my dad put it. Security against the storm. But I couldn't imagine that Emily and Bob had a retirement plan or even a 401K with their jobs. They certainly weren't sitting around bemoaning the fact.

Were they brave and carefree? Or foolish?

Their house was so small and common, yet it was nice. I loved being at the cottage with Jake. I could see living in a place like that, assuming I had a job and savings account and the rest of the package. But the cottage, though not huge, probably cost a couple of mil due to location. It wasn't exactly a sacrifice. Could I live in a place like Bob and Emily's?

The image of their fridge door flashed through my mind. There was love in that tiny house. Food. Heat in the winter and AC in the summer. And, as Emily said, it was less to worry about and take care of than a big place. Maybe living like that wouldn't be so bad.

But I knew I was kidding myself. I'd grown up with so much space, everything top of the line. My bedroom suite was larger than their living room and kitchen combined. I was probably being totally naive about how well I'd cope with less. It wasn't that I had to have fancy things. I didn't care about designer clothes or china or jewelry or things like that. But I did like my tech toys. And the idea of not being able to afford something I truly *needed*, or my family needed, made my stomach churn.

"Andy's going to Harvard Law School," Jake put in.

I snapped back to the conversation. Everyone was looking at me. I nodded. "Yeah. August twenty-fourth."

"Holy cow!" Bob sounded impressed. "I bet that's super hard to get into, right?"

"Hell yeah!" Jake enthused. "But Andy's always gotten straight As. The bum."

"What kind of law are you going to study?" Emily asked.

"Corporate law. Contracts. Domestic."

The phrases were as familiar to me as the days of the week. I remembered sitting at the mahogany dining room table in our house, brochures spread out all over, talking about specializations in law. My mom had even joined us the first time, being the household attorney. I'd been interested in international law, but my dad wasn't a fan. He said too many people went into it because it sounded glamorous, but these days it was hardly necessary for a lawyer to leave his office no matter where the contract parties were. And my mom said there was way more work in domestic contracts and mergers, and that international law was complex enough that corporations usually hired off-shore specialists to deal with it.

"What about you, Jake?" Emily asked.

"I'm starting a job in September as a software engineer in California." Jake's voice was warm. "Nerd for hire, basically."

"You guys have it all mapped out," Bob said without a trace of envy.

Was that because he couldn't imagine such things for himself? Or because he was content with the life he had? And why did I always have to think about such things? Bob and Emily's life was none of my business. There were millions of people who got on just fine without my input—or my dad's.

"Yeah, sounds like you both have great futures ahead of you," Emily said.

"Except we won't be together anymore," I said, without thinking. My voice came out bitter. I took a long swig of my beer, holding it carefully between my two bandaged mitts and resisting the urge to clench my fists.

Why did I say that? That was obvious, wasn't it? And no one cared.

Emily gave me a sad look. "You guys are great friends. I'm sure you'll keep in touch. I still have lunch once a month with my BFF from high school."

I forced a smile. "Sure. We definitely will." I had to change the subject before the sudden nervous energy in my body made me do or say something stupid. "Tell me about this boat, Bob. Did you fix it up?"

"Oh, Lord. What did we pay for this thing? Like three hundred bucks?" Bob asked Emily. He proceeded to describe the state it had been in when they got it. I nodded my head where appropriate, half wondering why anyone would do all the work he was describing instead of just buying a new boat. When Jake shifted in his chair and his foot ended up resting against mine, neither of us moved.

Back at the house, Bob put steaks on the grill, and Emily got us set up at an old picnic table on the back deck with a couple of fresh beers and a big bowl of corn chips. Jake and I were used to grabbing a chip between two bandaged hands and getting it to our mouths. It wasn't pretty, but it was functional. But that wasn't something I was prepared to do in front of others. We both ignored the chips.

When the meal was served, Emily and Bob sat on one side of the table and Jake and I were on the other. It was so . . . couple-y. Did Emily know about us? Or suspect? She and Bob touched constantly—his hand on her neck, her hand on his thigh, or he'd brush his nose through her hair. They talked about plans for the baby. They talked about the summer heat and places they'd taken the boat.

For the first time, my brain started down a new pathway. Uncharted territory. I'd thought about Jake and gay sex when he'd started seeing Kevin. Then I'd thought about Jake and gay sex and *me*, all happening simultaneously. We did that now. We did that a *lot*. But it was still like . . . bros getting each other off. It didn't affect anything outside the bedroom. And inside the bedroom we weren't exactly lovey-dovey. It was casual and, well, goal oriented.

For the first time, I questioned that. I tried to imagine myself and Jake here as a couple. Being . . . couple-y, like Bob and Emily. Holding hands. Giving each other brief kisses. Jake's hand on my thigh. The feel of his warm hair under my chin. I thought about the relaxed comfort of being together, of being as together as two people could possibly be. It wasn't hard to imagine. In fact, it was a little terrifying how close to that we already were. Jake was my best friend in the world, my shadow, the person I could happily spend all my time with. And we were also having sex. How was that substantively different than being a couple? The lawyer in me knew it wouldn't hold up in court.

But Jake will be leaving in a few weeks, my brain reminded me, *so we're not that and never will be.* Immediately, my gut twisted.

What if not, though? What if . . . what if Jake and I were there, as a couple, with no discernable event horizon? Just living our lives, together, with no expiration date?

My chest felt tight and heavy. That would be weird. That wasn't what I wanted. That wasn't my future. I knew exactly what my future looked like, and that wasn't it. Being in a gay relationship, permanently? That wasn't me. Even if I could accept that for myself, outside of any social, biological, or fiscal concerns, I couldn't visualize being "out" with Jake as my partner in front of the world.

I wasn't that guy, someone everyone knew was gay, someone whose life was defined like that, limited by those parameters. The idea felt wrong. And then the idea of living in a dumpy little house on a hill like this. That wasn't my fate either. It might look okay now, on a gorgeous sunny day, when Bob and Emily had company and were all cheerful. But what happened if the baby came and it was sick? What if the house flooded? Or slid down the hill? Did they have insurance for that? What if one of them lost their job? What if they started to hate each other because there was too much need and not enough fuel to slake it?

"Do you have a personal vendetta against pasta salad?" Jake asked me curiously.

I stopped stabbing at my plate with the wrist tool. "Sorry. I was thinking about something else."

"The end of the world as we know it?" Jake guessed.

"Idiot," I muttered under my breath affectionately. I wanted to press my thigh against his, just as a . . . I didn't know. Warning? A silent laugh? But I didn't. Because we weren't a couple.

When Emily dropped us off at the cottage, it was only nine o'clock. But I wasn't in the mood to fool around for once, too much on my mind, and I guessed Jake wasn't either. He was quieter than usual. He headed off to the bedroom with a simple "Good night."

We'd never slept in the same bed at the cottage, but that night I was tempted to go to his room and ask if I could sleep there. I felt empty inside, hollow, and it wasn't a good ache. It was like a toothache. In my soul. My soul had a toothache, and both of my hands were burned. Great.

It took me a long time to fall asleep.

Chapter
THIRTEEN

JAKE

On a Friday night in mid-July, Andy and I took a huge bowl of popcorn Emily had left for us and headed into the living room to watch a movie. We'd had Bob hook up an old laptop of Andy's to the big-screen TV so we could control browsing by voice.

We paged through lists of options on Netflix.

"There." I nodded my chin at the screen. "*Love Actually*. Let's watch that."

Andy groaned. "Are you kidding me? Why don't you just stick a fork in my eye?"

"Oh, is that too chick flick for you, Mr. Manly Man? We've watched every Marvel, zombie, and Bond movie twice now. I'm ready for something that doesn't involve Spandex or eating brains, and I swear if you get that Bond theme in my head again, I'll have to hurt you."

"Fine, but there are other options. What about a TV series?"

"What about *Love Actually*? It's supposed to be funny, and I've never seen it. Everyone talks about it. It's a gap in your pop-culture education if you haven't watched it at least once."

"I never watched *Little Mermaid* either," Andy pointed out.

"Well maybe you should!" I teased. "I've heard there's some deep subtext in that."

Andy scooped up a few kernels of popcorn with his mitt and tossed them at my face. "Ha-ha."

"Come on, let's try it. If we don't like it, we can turn it off."

"Yeah, okay," he grumbled. But I could tell he was objecting just because he thought he should.

We started the movie. It wasn't bad. Pretty funny, really, with all those awkward, pining couples. Andy and I laughed at the bit about the porn movie stand-ins. But the movie gave me the feels, which was embarrassing. I couldn't help the longing, though, especially with Andy slouched on the couch next to me. The sun went down outside, and the movie played on, now the only glow in the room.

The kissing scene between Laura Linney and Rodrigo Santoro . . . God, it was so passionate. It hurt my chest. I rubbed at my sternum absently with my wrist. I realized this movie had been a bad idea after all. *Note to self: no more romances for the rest of the summer.* I couldn't go there. It made me want things, feel things, that were epically impossible. Like a life with Andy. Like some awkward-yet-brave confession of love and then things magically working out. Goddamn it.

As soon as the movie was over, I stood up and faked a yawn. "Man, I'm wiped. I'm goin' to bed."

"Wait a minute." Andy looked up at me from the couch, his face pursed in a frown.

"What?"

"Sit down a second."

I didn't want to, but if I resisted, he'd want to know why. So I went over and flicked up the light switch, hoping the glare would chase away what I was feeling. Then I sat back down on the couch. "So?"

"Hey, um . . . that movie reminded me of something I've been thinking about . . ."

I waited, no clue where Andy was going with this. He gave me a sheepish smile. "I thought we might try expanding our repertoire."

"What? What do you mean?" The back of my neck felt damp all of a sudden, and the butterflies in my stomach swarmed up as though his words had been the blast of a shotgun. Was he talking about sex? He had to be, right? What did he mean by "expanding our repertoire"? Since that day in the kitchen when I'd rimmed him, I'd tried hard to keep it just about getting off. Was he bored?

Andy licked his lips nervously. He was studying my face as if wary of my reaction. "I thought we might mix it up a bit. Like . . . we could try making out."

I stared at him, unable to believe my own ears. "Making out?" I parroted like an idiot.

"Yeah, Jake. *Making out.*" There was a glimmer of amusement in his eyes now, but also more wariness. He folded his arms across his chest.

My brain felt like a clothes dryer full of tennis balls on the spin cycle. *Why would he want to make out? He means, like, kiss? Is he talking about kissing? He wants to kiss me? Why? There's no logical reason for that. I mean, if it's just about getting off because of our hands . . .*

Sure I wanted to kiss *him*. Badly. Could he feel the same way?

But why? My brain insisted.

"But why?" my mouth said. I cringed. I shouldn't be making a big deal out of this, but I had to know.

He raised his eyebrows. "Because . . . I like making out?" he said, like I was being purposefully obtuse.

"But . . . me?" I managed, squeaking a bit. Great. I sounded like I'd inhaled helium.

Andy looked around. "Who do you think I'm talking to, Jake? You think I want to make out with the drapes? What's the big deal? We've done a hell of a lot more than that. I mean, you've been swallowing my come for weeks now. Would it be that gross to kiss me?" His tone calmed me down. Not because of the jokey arrogance in it, but because of the insecurity underneath.

A lot of our friends swore Andy was never insecure about anything. But that wasn't true. We'd shared late-night conversations about how he worried about living up to his dad's expectations, about not being sure what he wanted, if he was good enough, smart enough, fast enough, talented enough. He was—all of those things, and I always told him so. He did the same for me when my ass was dragging. But right now I could hear his insecurity. Did he think I'd make fun of him for saying he liked to make out?

I hurried to reassure him. "No, that's not it. I've done way grosser things than kissing you. There was that whole caterpillar thing," I joked.

He didn't smile. He looked at me, biting his lip. "So?"

"I don't know if it's such a great idea." I swallowed, desperately wanting to step back, step away from the couch and him, put more space between us. *Don't ask me to do this.*

I already was way too invested. If we started that, started kissing and touching like real lovers, how the hell was I supposed to walk away at the end of the summer? We had no possible future, even if Andy wanted one with me, which he didn't. He might be less "all straight all the time" than I'd previously thought, but he was still *mostly* straight. This thing between us was only because of our current, totally bizarre and isolated situation. I had to cling to that. I couldn't forget it.

He must have read the longing on my face, because he suddenly leaned back and put his arms across the back of the sofa, his face relaxed into a cocky smile. "Dare you, Jake. Come on. I dare you to kiss me. Tongue and all."

Fucker. My blood thundered in my ears. There might be a universe where Jake Masterson could resist Andy Tyler, but it wasn't this one.

"I hate you," I said. "With the power of a thousand Foo Fighters concert amps."

Andy blew me a sarcastic air-kiss. "Liar. You love me to pieces. Come and get it, baby."

I laughed, but my body responded to the starting gun before I was even aware I'd agreed to the race. I found myself with a knee on the couch between Andy's legs. He reached up to place a wrist on my hip, pulling me down toward him. His face was suddenly serious. I leaned down, my heart thudding. One part of my brain was still screaming that I shouldn't do this. But it wasn't loud enough to stop me.

"I hate you," I muttered again just before my lips met his.

What are we doing? The thought echoed around my head, alarm bells clanging. But the noise got dimmer and dimmer as we sank into the kiss, tentative at first, and then not so much. Andy had a wide, hot mouth and his lips were firm. His chin was just a bit scratchy with end-of-day stubble. He sucked at me lightly, the tip of his tongue against my lips until I opened up. At the first taste of him—salty like the sound and vaguely popcorn flavored—I shivered. It was a totally involuntary spasm, head to toe. Andy made a whimpery little sound in his throat in response. He tugged, and I shifted until I was kneeling on the couch, my knees spread around his hips. We never broke the kiss. I couldn't have moved away from his lips if the cottage had caught on fire.

Come to think of it, the cottage *was* on fire. Or maybe it was just me.

I sat on Andy's thighs. He put both his arms around me, hugging me close to his chest, his forearms and wrists firm on my back, his tongue hot and slick in my mouth, sweet and sensuous, perfect suction tugging at me. It felt like every nerve in my body was directly connected to that spot, and it had a secret hotlink to my heart as well.

God, I regretted his damaged hands just then. He was kissing me, and I wanted to feel his palms, his big hands and long fingers pressed against me. And, fuck, not being able to use *my* hands was a tragedy on par with the bloodiest things Shakespeare ever wrote. I wanted to touch Andy's neck. I wanted to lose my fingers in his hair, brush my thumb along that gorgeous jaw of his as his tongue was in my mouth.

I groaned, desire and frustration bubbling out of me. I wanted to crawl inside him. I wanted to sink to the floor and die because it would never be enough.

Andy turned his head to the side, breaking the kiss. He stared at me, his eyes wide, his pupils huge, swallowing up the blue the way lust was swallowing me. I'd never felt like this before—my emotions so raw, physical need so thick in my body I could swear my actual blood had heated. At that moment, Andy was a black-and-white necessity to me, like air. Denise, Jeanette, Kevin . . . everyone I'd ever been with before all faded away into nothing.

Did Andy feel anything like what I felt when we kissed?

My nerves got the better of me and a joke burst out. "Wow, you have a dirty tongue. You talk to your mother with that mouth?"

He smirked. "You're the one who rimmed me."

Oh, so we were not pretending that hadn't happened? Damn. I nodded, my face burning. "Emily put something in the sandwich that day. Some kind of psychedelic, I'm pretty sure."

"Jake." Andy's face grew serious.

My chest thudded like a badly played set of drums.

"Can we . . . maybe . . . go to bed and kiss? You're fucking making me lightheaded." He attempted a laugh like he was kidding, but I didn't think he was. God knew, *I* was lightheaded.

I looked for some sign on his face that this meant something to him, but he wouldn't meet my eyes. And then I wanted to kick my own ass for wanting that.

"Yeah. Let's go." I managed to worm my way off the couch, Andy helping me with his elbows.

We went down the hall. I was in the lead, and I paused by his bedroom door. "Which room?"

"Mine. Better bed."

I went in and he followed, not bothering to turn on the light. I had a momentary worry. Were we going to *bed* bed? Or just having sex? Should I put my PJ bottoms on?

We'd never slept together at the cottage before. Why did it feel like kissing changed everything? It didn't. It changed nothing.

Andy sat down on the bed, not turning down the covers. "C'mere."

I couldn't make out his expression in the dim light. That was fine. Good probably. I knelt on the bed, and we worked around until we were lying side by side. My heart continued to pound like there was a predator in the room. But if there was a dangerous beast, it was inside me. Hope, maybe.

Andy leaned toward me and our lips met. It felt even bigger this time around, more like a choice. More like a statement. We were crossing a line that was more significant than any stunt we'd dared before.

He pressed me back and partially lay on top of me. And, oh fuck, that felt good. I wriggled under him, wanting him to press me down, cover me all the way. He obliged, scooting onto me, bringing our hips and chests into alignment, his mouth still hot on mine.

He was rigid in his shorts, as rigid as it was possible to be. *Do I really turn him on?* I wondered for the hundredth time. Or was he just horny by nature? Hell, I couldn't be bothered to think right then, not when he ground against me. His shaft rubbed over mine through two pairs of the silky gym shorts we were living in this summer. It was the sexiest, raunchiest thing ever. Pleasure pulsed through my cock, and my balls drew in, that awesome tightening coil. I made an embarrassing noise into his mouth.

He did it again and pulled away from my lips, sucking at my jaw, my neck, licking my ear. That was all new territory. I wanted to do the same to him, but I didn't want to get in his way. I grabbed his hips the best I could with my wrists, needing to keep him there.

"*Andy.*" My face burned at the sheer desperation in my voice.

"God, this feels good. Why does it feel so good?" Andy sucked at my throat.

Oh thank God. He feels it too. "Because I'm just that hot?" I hooked my calves around his thighs, opening myself up, unable to resist. And then he was pushing into me at the base of my dick and balls. Dear God. What would it be like to have him fuck me?

Lust shot another hot gush through me. My entire body was heavy and full and oh-so close to coming.

He made another sexy moan and attacked my mouth again, his thrusting hips tormenting me. Then there was nothing but his mouth and the escalating pressure. His thrusts got faster, grinding harder. I wasn't going to be able to stop. Didn't want to.

I broke away from his lips long enough to gasp. "Gonna come."

He made a noise of agreement and took my mouth again. His tongue plunged deep inside me as I began to shake. My eyes squeezed shut. The orgasm was like a freight train. My body clenched tight, only held to the Earth by his weight on top of me.

He made a strangled gasp in my ear and tensed against me. I felt his dick jerk against mine as he pulsed. Oh hell. That was hot, even better than when he was in my mouth, because in this position we could have been lovers.

After a while, when all that remained was the sound of our ragged breathing, he rolled to the side and shuffled until he lay on his back. His shoulder was still pressed against mine. I stared up at the ceiling.

Damn it. Fuckity, fuck, fuck, fuck. I was so head over heels in love with him.

"Wanna sleep here tonight?" he asked, his voice thick.

"Okay." Sleep sounded like a safe refuge. My eyelids were heavy and my body totally buzzed from coming so hard. Most of all, I didn't want to think about the day this would all be over.

I scooted out of my gym shorts though, because they were sticky with come. "I feel bad for Emily having to do our laundry. I may never be able to look her in the face again."

Andy grunted in agreement. "Maybe we can invent a story about spilled ice cream or something."

"Yeah, she's pregnant, bro. I think she's gonna know come when she sees it."

We both got naked, leaving our soiled clothes on the floor, and crawled under the covers. Andy turned his back to me and went to sleep instantly. But I lay awake for a long time, thinking about kissing him and worrying about how much of a train wreck this was going to be in the end.

ANDY

I wanted to kiss Jake all the time. *I mean, all the time.* It was pathetic. And a little bit scary. Not that I had much to distract me at the cabin. And we were together twenty-four seven. But still. I shouldn't want him like that. Shouldn't crave it. It was dangerous, and not in a good way either. The danger felt like a worm I'd swallowed, some flesh-devouring parasite that had moved into my stomach to eat me up from the inside.

We'd be sitting on the dock, watching boats go by and browning in the sun despite the thirty SPF lotion Walter slathered on us every morning. And I'd glance at Jake and want badly to lean over and taste the bead of sweat on his lip.

Or we'd be in the kitchen rummaging around getting into one of Emily's precooked meals, and I'd have an almost uncontrollable urge to back him into the counter and kiss him until we were both coming in our shorts.

Or we'd be watching TV on the couch and I'd want to lie down with him against me as we watched.

I didn't do any of those things. We were still having sex at least twice a day. And once we agreed that was what we were doing, and moved into one of the bedrooms, all the walls fell. We always kissed, it was the first thing we did, and we kept kissing all the way through sex unless one or both of us moved to do oral. But most of the time we didn't sixty-nine anymore. Mostly we rubbed off against each other because that way we could keep kissing.

That was fucked up, right? What guy preferred a dry hump to a blowjob? But I did. I was starved for his mouth. A blowjob was a blowjob, and Jake's were particularly fine, but kissing him was . . . intense. It soothed that itchy place inside me. I loved the way his tongue moved against mine, *Jake's tongue, Jake's mouth*. It ramped me up like nothing else I'd ever experienced. Maybe because I knew I *shouldn't* want it. I shouldn't want to kiss Jake, press against him, be that close to him, that in tune. That was way gayer than a blowjob. But knowing I shouldn't want it made me want it all the more.

Still we kept it to the bedroom. Only the bedroom.

Then one night we were watching a *House of Cards* marathon, relaxed on the couch. My arm went over the sofa. Jake scooted closer after putting down the remote, and my mitt rested on his shoulder. Next thing I knew, he was nuzzling my neck, and I got incredibly turned on. But there was no rush. We'd already gotten off twice that day. So we kissed a little and watched the show some more. I sucked on his ear, making him groan. He threw his leg over mine and ground his thigh now and then against my dick.

My heart pounded, knowing we were crossing another line. This wasn't even about getting off, not really. But I didn't want to stop.

After that, we touched and kissed most of the time while watching TV.

We didn't talk about it. Of course, we *talked*, we talked about all kinds of shit. But we didn't talk about what we were doing. We didn't talk about what we were to each other. And we didn't talk about the fact that it was almost August, and we were looking at the end of the summer the way a guy looked into the barrel of a mugger's gun.

Dare
#4

Chapter
FOURTEEN

JAKE

It was the end of July, and Andy and I had a doctor's appointment. Walter had been doing a great job, and he acted pleased with our progress, but it was time for another formal checkup. On July twenty-first, he drove us to a doctor's office in Barnstable.

Dr. Gallaway's practice was in an upscale complex, and he was a soft-spoken man in his fifties. It was our third visit that summer, and the previous times he'd basically said "keep doing what you're doing" and "keep the bandages on." Andy's dad's insurance magically covered it somehow, even me. Maybe the doctor had agreed to a "twofer" since he only had to check our hands, and mine were in a similar state to Andy's.

But that visit he unwrapped Andy's hands, then mine, and examined each one carefully, holding them under a light and pressing gently on the skin.

The burns seemed healed to me. My palms and fingers were only slightly puffy, the skin that had been an angry red was now light pink, and the edges of the burn were hard to see. The texture of the skin was better too. It looked thicker, more like normal skin and less like a fragile membrane.

"This is good. This is good," Dr. Gallaway muttered as he peered at Andy's palm intently. He looked up at Andy's face. "Any pain?"

"Not much. Only if I try to lift something heavy with my mitts. Or try to stretch my fingers. The skin is still itchy, but not as bad as it was."

"Good, good." Dr. Gallaway looked at me. "What about you, Jake?"

"What he said, pretty much. He's always copying me. It's so annoying."

Andy nudged me with his shoulder, and Dr. Galloway smiled at the joke. "Well, in this case, copying is good."

In the past few weeks, we'd been able to use our hands more. Even though they were still bandaged, the pain had lessened to the point where we could pick things up between our palms and push and pull things like chairs. We could stroke each other's back and hips, the bandages slightly scratchy and shiver-inducing.

Yeah, I didn't think Dr. Gallaway would be interested in hearing about that.

"Um-hmm. Um-hmm." He turned off the light and straightened up. "I think you boys are ready to leave the bandages off. But that doesn't mean a free for all. Let pain be your guide. I wouldn't try lifting anything heavy—no barbells, boxes, nothing like that. You can do light tasks again. Bathing is fine, doing dishes, getting dressed on your own. That sort of thing."

"Jet skiing?" Andy suggested hopefully.

Dr. Gallaway laughed. "If you can stand the cold of the sound, sure. Don't grip the handlebars too tightly or, better yet, wear gloves. But no lifting the thing in and out of the water."

"We can get someone to do that part for us." Andy smiled at me.

"The new skin is tender from the bandages and ointment, but the fresh air will toughen it up. In two more weeks, you should be pretty much back to normal. For now, proceed with a bit of caution. Okay?"

Dr. Gallaway smiled and held out his hand to me. I shook it. His grasp was light, but it was still a privilege just to be able to shake hands again. Imagine that! And on the way out of the office, I could actually open and close doors without needing to use my wrists or fumble around like a bandaged freak.

I supposed one of us could have driven, but Walter had brought us in his car, so I got into the back seat and Andy took the passenger side like before. Walter congratulated us, thanking God for our recovery and all of that. I was excited and happy. I kept turning my hands front to back and looking at them with wonder. Talk about taking something for granted! I would never, ever be less than appreciative for the ability to text, type, or eat with a real spoon. I didn't have any permanent scarring at all. *Damn*, we were so lucky.

But every time I looked at Andy on the drive home, he was staring out the window, his face blank.

And then it struck me, and my heart crashed from the sky like Icarus on his waxy wings.

We had no excuse to touch each other anymore.

ANDY

That afternoon when we got back from the doctor's appointment with our unwrapped hands, Jake wouldn't meet my eyes. We both got a drink from the fridge, not saying a word. Then he got out the Xbox and controllers and started setting it up on the big TV.

"I'm going to play some *Halo*. You want to play?" he asked me, almost like an afterthought. He still didn't look at me.

"Nah," I said. "Go ahead."

I went out the back door of the cottage. I needed time to myself, and it seemed like Jake did too. I wanted to take the jet ski out, but I didn't want to bug Emily or Bob to come over and get it out of the shed. Tomorrow morning would be soon enough. But I had to do something physical. I ended up batting around a badminton birdie because it was light and the task was mindless and didn't hurt my hands.

God, I missed real sports. I longed to feel a bat in my hands again, feel the jarring crack of a softball as I slammed into it, to feel the weight and speed of a spinning football as I caught it. To swim without worrying about infection or bandages.

To touch Jake.

No, not that. I'd gained the freedom to do everything else, but I'd lost that. It had been taken from me.

Had it? What would Jake do if I suggested we keep fooling around?

I thought it through as I bumped that stupid birdie up into the air over and over again. Tried to see the logic on both sides.

We'd started messing around because, with our bandaged hands, we couldn't get ourselves off. Fact.

We both liked it. Fact.

So why not continue even though the bandages were gone?

But the clenching in my gut—the worry and the weird—was also a fact. The bandages had been a great excuse to try things out with Jake and pretend it didn't mean anything. If we kept fooling around now, it would be different. Despite the sensitivity of my palms, I was pretty sure I could get myself off. Or, hell, now that we looked more or less normal, we could go to a club. There were a half-dozen hopping night spots within easy driving distance along the sound. Jake and I had been to most of them before, together, and picked up girls in years past.

So if we continued to have sex now, I'd be admitting that I wanted Jake, specifically, that I wanted him as a sexual partner. And I *did*. But . . . did I really? Or had it just become a convenient habit, like continuing to eat the bowl of nuts because it was in front of you? And if I *did* want Jake, what did that mean?

That was the hard part. I did want to keep touching Jake, kissing Jake, getting off with Jake. The thought of stopping was painful. But now it would mean something, and I didn't know how that could work. In a few weeks, we'd be going our separate ways. I'd be meeting girls at Harvard, dating girls. And Jake would probably date girls in California too. Or maybe he'd find someone like Kevin.

If we were still lovers, all that would be weird. Would Jake expect me to be monogamous? A long-distance relationship was hard enough; I'd tried that and failed with Kristen my senior year of high school. But a long-distance relationship with a guy? With a *friends-with-bennies* guy? How would that even work? And why? Or would we just be best friends who might fool around if and when we happened to see each other? It was too murky and undefined, too weird.

It would be best to stop now. This would be the cleanest break. Right now, at this moment, and for this reason: the bandages are off.

I knew that. I knew it would be the best place to get off this crazy train before Jake was hurt or I was hurt or something happened to ruin our friendship. But I didn't want to. I really didn't want to.

Batting the bird around for another hour didn't bring me any further insight. I figured I'd try to suss out what Jake wanted. If he made the first move . . .

But he didn't. When I went back inside, he was in his room with the door shut. He came out a few hours later, and we ate the dinner Emily had left, but he avoided looking at me for very long, and he chatted about some science article he'd been reading online about nanotechnology. After dinner, he said he was wiped and was going to read in his room for a bit and go to sleep early. I said that was cool, that I'd probably watch a movie.

I watched *The Babadook* on Netflix, and sent him a text that I was starting it. But he never came out of his room.

It's for the best, I told myself. *He wants a clean break too. It's for the best.*

Maybe if I repeated it often enough, I'd believe it.

Chapter
FIFTEEN

Jake

From the back of the cottage, we could walk or run for miles along the beach, past other cottages and big estates. At two miles, we crossed through a preserved wetlands with boardwalks that spanned the channels that ran into the sea and were slippery under our shoes from the humid air. We passed low, peach-colored cliffs and long rocky promontories. The landscape was dominated by the vast water that stretched to the horizon, the open sky, the tawny sand, and the endless movement of the waves.

After the bandages came off, we started running again, as if reminded that we were no longer invalids. The blood didn't pound in my palms anymore, and running didn't painfully jar my hands, though I kept them limp at the end of bent elbows to minimize the impact.

And maybe running was a way to take out our frustrations. I didn't bring up sex once the bandages had come off, and Andy didn't either. For the first few days, it was the elephant in the room. I didn't want to suggest we go to the bedroom and get off, because then it would be clear that I wanted sex *with him*, not just sex. But if he'd brought it up, I would have been happy to continue. Maybe he felt the same way—I didn't know, but he didn't mention it. And after the first few days, it was definitely too awkward to broach the subject.

We said our good-byes to Walter, since he wasn't needed anymore. Emily continued to come by in the mornings, bringing us meals and straightening up, though there was less for her to do now. Andy took long showers, and I wondered if he was jerking off in there. I wondered if it was just as good for him as when we'd been together. I feared the answer.

I missed kissing Andy most of all—especially kissing while being pressed against each other. I wanted to never forget how that felt. But holding on to a memory was as practical as holding on to a fistful of sand.

Bob put the best two jet skis at the dock. I was sort of depressed and didn't want to go out much, but Andy took off on his and would be gone for hours. I considered calling my mom and having her pick me up. After all, I no longer needed help, and it might be easier not to see Andy at all. I had to start getting over this sense of crushing disappointment. But I couldn't do it. The cottage on the sound was such an idyllic place, and I'd probably never see it again. And I didn't want to give up being with Andy either, even if I couldn't touch him. He was still my best friend. And our separation would come soon enough.

Two weeks after our bandages came off, we were coming back from a long run along the beach when Andy's cell phone buzzed. He carefully got it out of his running belt, his fingers still a bit tender, like mine were. I could see the caller ID was *Dad*.

He gave me a worried smile and moved away from the water, far enough away to have some privacy. He kicked at a log and answered his phone, his body rigid with tension. We both knew what the call was about. It was like getting a call from the executioner.

I did leg stretches while Andy was busy in order to stay warmed up, even though we were nearly back at the cottage. Despite our six-mile-plus run, I was suddenly filled with the need to take off. Flight instinct, maybe.

I stared at the water, watching the foamy waves wash the shore. The ocean had existed before Andy and I were born, and it would be there long after we were dust. It didn't care about our drama. I wished I could borrow a bit of that objectivity. But my stomach was tied in knots. The sea might not care about our drama, but I did.

Andy hung up and walked back over to me. He didn't meet my eyes, merely jerked his head and started walking toward the cottage. I followed.

"Well?" I prompted.

Andy still wouldn't look at me. He ran both hands through his hair, as though he'd missed expressing himself in that tactile way, but he said nothing.

"I swear to God, I will hurt you if you don't tell me what he said," I teased half-heartedly.

Andy grimaced. "My dad's coming to pick us up on the eighteenth. That's a Friday, two weeks from today."

My blood chilled in my veins, despite the humid summer heat. "But... I thought you said your classes didn't start until August thirty-first."

"Yes, but orientation starts the twenty-fourth, and my dad wants the weekend before to go over the curriculum, get books and whatever else I need, and to help me move into the campus housing." Andy's Adam's apple bobbed as he swallowed. There was a ragged edge to his voice.

"Oh."

It couldn't be so soon. The summer was supposed to include August, *all* of it. But reality didn't give a toss about my ideas of "summer," apparently. It suddenly occurred to me that this wasn't just about Andy. My own life was about to go into free fall as well. I felt slightly sick. "Right. Um . . . can you guys drop me off at my house on Friday? Or I can have my mom pick me up at yours."

"We'll drop you off."

I should be glad. My invalid period was coming to an end. Hell, there was no reason to hang out at my mom's house when we got back either. Sierra was anxious for me to get to California. She was getting married in late September and "needed my help." Plus my hands were healed enough to type. I could fly right on to San Jose and start my job two weeks early. God knew, I could use the money, and it would show Neverware I had initiative.

But the current state of my initiative was MIA. I glanced at Andy's profile as we walked, and thought that, perhaps, I wanted to die. He was everything I'd ever wanted, or ever would want, in a partner. We had a shared history. He was the most beautiful person on earth to me—not to anyone else, perhaps, but he was to me. We fit together so easily and so well. We never got tired of each other's company. I made him laugh. He made me brave. The sex had been incredible—as natural as touching myself and, at the same time, as hot as I could ever imagine.

I'd been with him like that after wanting him for years and giving up hope. And now I had to give up hope all over again.

Fuck it. I should have stood my ground and refused when he'd first suggested getting each other off. Then my heart wouldn't be breaking right now. But part of me knew that I'd make the same decision in a heartbeat if I had the chance.

We reached the cottage, left the beach, and went up the few stone steps to the lawn. Andy paused at the back door and finally looked at me. The emotion in his eyes surprised me. I guess I expected . . . resignation? A shade of regret? Or, hell, maybe he was thrilled to be moving on with his life, getting to Harvard. It was *fucking Harvard* after all. Of course he was excited. But, instead, what I saw in his eyes was a dangerous sparkle.

Uh-oh. I knew that look. That was Andy's reckless, throw-himself-onto-the-fire expression.

"No," I said immediately, taking a step back on the grass. "Christ, we just got healed from your last stunt! I don't even want to hear it."

"Oh, you want to hear it," Andy assured me in a dark voice. He glanced around, as if to make sure we were alone. But there was no one close by on the beach, and the neighboring houses were hidden by scrubby trees on either side of the property.

"You promised no more stunts," I reminded him. "And we promised our folks. Ding, ding! Oh, look, it's the reality bell! And it's calling your name, Andrew Tyler."

Andy didn't respond to my sarcasm. His intensity never faltered. "This isn't dangerous. At least not that way. I want . . ." He swallowed, then spoke firmly. "I want us to fuck. I want us to fuck each other."

I gaped at him, blinking. Okay. That was not what I'd been expecting. "Um . . . *What?*"

"You heard me."

"Why? There'll be plenty of girls for you to fuck when you get back to Boston," I said, sounding bitter.

"Jesus, Jake, I've fucked girls before, and I probably will again. That's not the point!"

"Then what *is* the point?" I nearly shouted at him.

Despite how intimate we'd been in weeks past, despite the hours we'd spent kissing, it was still a jolt when he reached over and took my hand in his. Would I ever get over Andy touching me? Probably not. I looked around again. I didn't care about people seeing us like this, but I figured Andy did.

As if reading my mind, he opened the back door of the cottage and pulled me inside. The AC was on, and it felt wonderful after the cloying, sticky heat outside. My shirt was plastered to me from the run, and I was so hot on the inside with a thousand conflicting emotions, I might melt into a puddle right there at the door.

"Just listen. All right?" Andy's face, his tone, were so serious I had no choice but to nod even though a small voice in my head warned me this conversation wouldn't end well.

He took a deep breath. "I know it started out as a way to get off. But . . ." He swallowed. "The thing is, I never really had the chance to experiment before."

I huffed in disbelief. "Are you kidding me? What about Amber and the two pairs of handcuffs? You were finding honey in weird places for a week. I even took to calling you Pooh Bear for a while!"

Andy laughed and groaned simultaneously. He tugged on his hair with his free hand as though he were in pain. "Stop being so cute!"

I blinked at him. He thought I was cute? I knew he thought I was funny. But *cute*?

He clenched his jaw and lowered his brow, giving me his stubborn look. "I'm serious. I want to know what it's like to fuck a guy! When am I ever going to get another chance? Who, besides you, would I ever trust enough to . . . to, God, Jake, to *kiss*, much less to do anal?"

I had no answer. I blinked in surprise.

Andy was so earnest as he went on, his voice dropping to soothing tones. "In two weeks, this whole break from reality is going to be over, and we won't see each other again for a while. This is our only chance, *my* only chance, to experiment like this. We can agree that once we leave here, it's done. All right? But until then . . ." He ran his hand up my arm and curled it around my neck loosely. His blue eyes were pleading. "I'm just laying it all out there. *Until then*, I want to do everything with you, try everything. That's what I want. So what do you want, Jake?"

What do I want? I stared at him stupidly.

What I wanted was to be with Andy forever, for us to be together, openly, in front of the world. I wanted to come home to him after work every day and hold him every night. I wanted to throw popcorn at each other while watching movies and join a soccer league on the weekends. I wanted to be there when he graduated from law school. I wanted not to have my heart shattered into a million pieces. I wanted not to be broken for however many years it was going to take me to get over this.

I couldn't have those things, though. And it wasn't fair. Andy didn't get to take every piece of me and then walk away.

And, suddenly, I was angry. "No," I said, my voice cold. I pulled back from him and folded my arms over my chest. "I'm not interested in being your fuck toy for the next two weeks. I'm not going there with you."

"Why not?" Andy shouted, his words sour as bile. "You went there with Kevin!"

I froze. My muscles locked up even while my heart started pounding in my ears. "You knew about Kevin?"

He waved a hand like it wasn't any big deal. "Yeah, bro. I'm not an idiot. You were sexing it up with Kevin. Did you do that with him? Did you let him fuck you?"

It was like Andy was trying to keep his words neutral, but there was a hurt that lay under them like broken glass under a tablecloth, like in one of Andy's stupid tricks.

Why would he be upset about that? I mean, I always figured he'd freak out about Kevin, but only because he'd think I'd been lusting after him too. But we'd been getting each other off for two months so . . . that probably wasn't the problem. I struggled to understand.

"Did you?" Andy asked again, his eyes bright. He could be so damn pushy. He took a step toward me, crowding me against the door.

I licked my lips. What could I say? Obviously, I had lied to him. "Are you pissed that I didn't tell you about Kevin?"

Andy frowned, but then he shrugged. "I don't know. It didn't exactly make me happy. Why didn't you tell me what was going on?"

I rubbed my hands over my face. The skin on my fingers was still sensitive, and low-voltage needles of sensation erupted when I put pressure on them. But at least I had the use of them. "Um . . . Well. I'm bisexual." I said the words with certainty, not wobbling at all.

Andy gave me a raised eyebrow as if to say *no shit*.

"But I thought if I told you, you might . . ." I took a shuddering breath. *Figure out I'm in love with you.* ". . . freak out. About our friendship. Or the state of the perpetually shrinking straight population, maybe. So . . ."

He didn't smile. I went on.

"I guess I was trying to figure out exactly where the line fell for me. My personal Kinsey bar code, as it were. I should have told you about it. Trusted you. I'm sorry." I felt the urge to joke about it, try to make him relax. I tapped my chest and faked a French accent. "Regret, she ees zee queen of my 'eart."

Andy snorted. "God, Jake. You're such an idiot."

I shrugged as if to say *What else is new?*

"So what happens when you get to California? Are you gonna date guys, and be out at work and everything?"

Good question. Andy was a bright guy. It had probably taken him five seconds to figure out what had taken me months to wrap my head around. In California, I'd be starting fresh, and in a liberal environment. I'd already decided I'd be open about my sexuality, and Sierra had confirmed it was no big deal at Neverware. "I'll come out, yeah. I like girls. I do. And maybe I'll meet the perfect girl, and that will be it. But if I end up with a guy, that's okay too."

But first I have to get over you. Which is going to be so damn hard. I didn't say it. What was the point?

"You don't actually have a preference?" Andy's voice was stiff.

I searched for the words to explain. "With a guy it's more relaxed. Less trying to figure out what the other person wants. Then again, being with a girl is easier in a lot of ways—being out in public, family expectations . . . I don't know, bro. We'll see who I meet."

"Yeah." Andy's voice was quiet, and his eyes dropped to the floor. His forehead was furrowed in thought. But then he looked up at me, his eyes burning again. "So did you do it with Kevin? Anal sex?"

I sighed. Nope. Andy wasn't going to let it go. "Yeah. Yes. Yes, I did. We did that."

"Which way? I mean, did you . . ."

"Kevin. He, uh, thought of himself as a top. So we only did it . . ." *Christ.* "I bottomed. Once. It was fine." I nodded stupidly.

Andy's gaze grew darker. "Just 'fine'? That's the descriptive word you choose for being fucked up the ass?"

I wanted to growl at him. Though, granted, *fine* was a lousy descriptive word in any circumstances, much less to illuminate the experience of having a large dick rammed up my backside. "Sorry if I'm being subtle. How about 'I don't really want to get into the hairy details with you'?"

"Screw that. Did you like it?" Andy insisted, taking another step closer.

I had, in fact, liked it. It was probably my favorite thing Kevin and I had done together. Kevin had used plenty of lube and done the whole fingers thing and there hadn't been any pain, just lots of new sensations. Extremely good new sensations. But afterward, I hadn't liked the disconnect between the intense vulnerability of being taken like that and how I'd felt about Kevin at the time. It happened toward the end of our relationship, when I was starting to find him annoying. Also, he'd been way too smug about the whole thing, the whole "I Have A Big Dick" 'tude. We hadn't done it again.

"Well?" Andy demanded.

"Jesus. Yes, I liked it. All right? It was . . . pretty hot and it felt amazing."

"I wanna try it," Andy said at once, his voice hitching. "I want to fuck you. You can do me too if you want. But I *have* to do you. I want to know what it's like. Don't you want to see if it'd be different with us? You must, Jake. You're just as curious as I am."

His words—talking about us fucking, the way his voice already trembled with lust—caused flames to lick up my spine, set my balls to boiling, and my swelling dick steered toward my stomach. My resolve crumpled to my feet, softly, like loose PJ bottoms when the elastic broke.

"Jesus, Andy."

"I dare you," Andy husked out, his pale-blue eyes lit with the fires of hell and burning into mine. "Jake Masterson. I. Dare. You."

Chapter SIXTEEN

ANDY

I knew I was pushing Jake. I knew I shouldn't, not about this. But I couldn't stop myself. There was that maddening, itchy feeling inside me, urging me on. At times like this, it felt like the inside of my head was going a thousand miles per hour, and if I didn't make my body move, accelerate, drive forward to match pace, my psyche would break away from my corporeal being, and I'd become completely unglued.

I was an explosion primed to go off, and I had to relieve the pressure.

It didn't take a Freudian analyst to detect the reason for my current anxiety—it was down to my dad's call. I was utterly torn at the idea of leaving the cottage in two weeks. Speaking to him had been like a dash of ice water in the face—his no-nonsense voice, his iteration of all the practical details, everything that needed to get done before I started Harvard. He'd been so black-and-white about how it was time to *get on with my life*, like he grudged me this summer at the cottage, like he'd done me a huge favor by agreeing to it. Like there had been any other option.

There was a massive disconnect between all of that and the way I felt anchored here, in this cottage on the sound with Jake. The thought of being torn away from it ached like I had stinging ants crawling inside me. It was inevitable, as unstoppable as time itself.

"Come on, Jake," I urged. "Let's fuck. Right now. You can do me or I can do you, I don't really care, but I want it." *I need it.* Jake's back was against the door, his hands flat on the wood, like he was a cornered rabbit. His face was conflicted. It would have been funny at another time, but now I just needed him so badly to agree, to want this too. I didn't understand why he was resisting. He said he'd liked it with Kevin, and I knew damned well Jake and I had great sexual chemistry. These past few weeks had been ridiculous trying to pretend we didn't want to go to bed together. He had to feel that too.

I closed the last bit of space between us, leaning my chest into his, and then my hips. He turned his jaw away from me, being a stubborn ass, but I reached up and turned it gently back. I kissed him, soft for a second, then dirty, wiping the flat of my tongue against his lips, pulling back when he tried to chase it. I did it again, tempting him.

He groaned. "God, I hate you." He hooked his arm around my neck so he could hold me still. He kissed me hard, almost brutally, not letting me tease.

I grabbed his hips and ground against him. I was already hard, thrumming with desperation-fueled desire and, if Jake was conflicted, his body was not. His hips arched against me, his prick like a stone. He spread his thighs, letting me sink deeper between them.

I broke away from his mouth long enough to say, "You want me to fuck you? Or—"

"Yeah." Jake went after my neck with his hot, greedy mouth. One hand stroked down to my ass to pull me harder against him in case I had any misconception about what he meant.

But I wanted more. "Say it. Tell me, Jake."

He tensed and grabbed my face in both of his hands. His brown eyes bored into mine. "I want you to fuck me, Andy."

"Because you're turned on?" I demanded, still pushing for the brass ring. *Goddamn it.*

"No, because I fucking *want* you," he grit out, almost angrily. "I always—" He stopped himself, swallowed. "I want to do this with you."

I felt a surge of elation. "Okay. Great. So let's do it."

I stepped back, grabbed one of his wrists, and pulled him along behind me. In my bedroom I had some lube I used for wanking, and there were two condoms in my wallet. I always carried a couple, but right now I wished I had a whole box. If I had my way, we wouldn't be coming up for air until August eighteenth.

We both stripped fast, sweaty T-shirts and shorts flying. It had been a hot day, and we were both grungy from the run. We could shower, but no way was I waiting for that. In fact, an extra twist of desire coiled in my gut as I looked at him. I *wanted* him like this—smelling strongly of sun and of Jake. Christ. I'd had no idea I had a sweat kink.

I grabbed my wallet from the dresser and tossed the two condom packets on the bed. Jake had the bottle of lube from the bedside table. We looked at each other, standing next to the bed, both naked and crazy hard.

"How do you want it?" Jake asked, his voice rough. He was trembling just a little. I'd never wanted anyone more in my life.

Fast and hard. That was how I wanted it. At least this first time.

"Get on all fours on the bed," I said, my tone more demanding than I'd intended.

Jake hesitated. "You have to prep me first."

I rolled my eyes. "No shit. I do know how to Google."

Jake's intensity faded as he grinned. "I would have loved to hear Siri's response to that question."

"Christ, Jake, get on your knees!" I grabbed the bottle of lube out of his hand. *My* hands were shaking too, like some pathetic virgin. And as much as I loved smart-ass Jake, I didn't want to see him right now. I wanted sexy Jake, panting and spread out in front of me like a buffet.

He got on his hands and knees on the bed and then went further, lowering onto his elbows and putting his head in his hands as if in surrender. I had to stop after popping the cap on the lube and just stare for a second. Damn, what a picture he made with his ass up high, his thighs spread. His shoulders looked so broad like that, his back muscled and his ass round and tight. I could see his balls hanging down and the brown furl of his hole. It was pornographic. And hot.

And, God, how much trust was he showing to open himself up for me like that?

"Move," Jake muttered, breaking me out of my stare.

Hell, yeah. I squeezed lube onto my fingers and moved close to him. I held him by the hip with one hand and with two fingers of the other, spread the lube up and down his entire crack, squeezing his balls and making them slippery, rubbing my thumb over his hole.

He made a noise, and his shoulders sank further into the bed.

Despite my earlier claim, I was nervous. I knew what to do technically, but I'd never done anal with a girl, and I didn't want to blow it and have to stop. I worked my thumb around, adding another shot of lube, until it could sink into him easily. He gasped and wiggled his hips, but it didn't appear to hurt. I pumped my thumb in and out of him for a while till it moved easily. Then I went to two fingers.

"Is this okay?" I asked him as he began to work himself back onto my hand, getting greedy.

"Yeah. Just do it now. I want your dick."

Those words coming out of his mouth were so wrong and so unexpected. They sent a thrill through my body. "You sure?" He still felt tight.

"Yeah. Come on, Andy. Don't be shy now."

It might have been a joke, except his voice was too wrecked. I ripped open the condom packet. My fingers felt weirdly numb, probably because all the blood in my body was in my penis.

I put more lube on the condom, then lined up, holding Jake's hip with one hand. "Wish I could kiss you right now," I said, then cringed at the words. I should be talking dirty like Jake, not all sentimental.

But Jake just looked over his shoulder at me, his eyes wild. "Me too. Later. Just—"

I sank in. The warm heat pulled me deeper like I was sinking into butter. He was soft and tight at the same time, sheathing me in perfect friction. I had to withdraw twice before I was able to thrust all the way inside him, as deep as I could go. He spread his legs more and tilted his hips. The next time I thrust into him, my sac slapped against his, a sensation so new and so shiver-inducing that I gasped a little. I did it again and again. Yet another new kink discovered. That felt *amazingly* filthy.

Jake moaned, his head buried in his arms. "Christ, don't stop," he said, his words muffled. "Don't stop, Andy. Don't stop. Don't—"

I leaned forward, grabbed his shoulders, and began to pound into him, knocking the words right out of his mouth. God, I'd missed this, the sensation of fucking someone, the act of penetration, of sinking into a channel that had no obstacles and no end. Fucking Jake was perfect—seeing my cock vanish between those small, tight cheeks, feeling the muscles of his thighs and the slap of my balls on his, hearing his steady stream of moans, knowing I could ride him hard and he would beg for more, that it would never be too much for him to handle.

He rose up on one arm so he could turn his head and watch. His face was flushed, his lips wet, his eyes dark chocolate. His other hand went to his dick, and he began jerking it in time with my thrusts.

I wondered for a second if I was supposed to do that for him, but he looked so sexy doing it himself, and I was too busy fucking him hard to be bothered to slow down or change position so I could touch him. I was riding a cresting wave that was bound to drop, bound to thrust me up and spill me out like flotsam on the shore. His thighs shook. His eyes lifted and met mine, a dare in them. *Now.*

We shipwrecked together, shuddering. His channel tightened spasmodically, almost painfully, around me. I felt every one of his pulses and lost track of where mine ended and his began.

When I could move again, I collapsed onto the bed, pulled off the condom, and dropped it carefully next to the bed. Jake flopped to his stomach beside me. It felt like my heart was going to pound out of my chest. I couldn't stop touching him, even now. The hand closest to him reached out, stroking his skin. He had really soft, supple skin with tiny freckles. It tasted salty-sweet, I knew, and I might be a little bit addicted. He shifted on his belly a few inches so his body was next to mine, touching all the way down. But his face was still turned away and it wasn't good enough. I rolled onto my side and tugged at him until he was facing me. The look in his eyes was too much, and maybe what was in mine was too much too. He lowered his eyelids as if to avoid the intimacy. I kissed him.

We kissed and kissed, softly, with no urgency except the desire to connect. We pressed together. I felt Jake's stomach meet mine on each breath. His soft dick lay on my thigh, and I liked it. His fingers traced patterns on my back. My heart hurt.

And, still, I held him.

Chapter
SEVENTEEN

October 2015 - Junior year at NYU
Andy

It was a Saturday night, or more specifically 2 a.m. on a Sunday morning, and a group of us were on the subway returning to NYU after visiting a club in Brooklyn to hear a band called Crimson Folly. Besides Jake and my girlfriend, Amber, there were three others—Jay, who was one of Amber's girlfriends, and two guy friends from our dorm who had come along. Daniel, with his light-brown skin and dreads, and Seb, a pale and freckled redhead, were sitting on either side of Jay, heavily flirting. They both obviously hoped to get lucky tonight, though whether they were competing or open to getting lucky together with Jay in a threesome wasn't clear. Not that I cared what they did.

We'd all been drinking, but the cold air outside the club and the fumes in the subway station had mostly sobered me up. And what the air didn't do, my body's chemistry did. I'd been worked up for days with that itchy, restless, rash-dash feeling prowling inside me like a caged beast. That inner turmoil seemed to affect my metabolism, because I'd barely felt the alcohol I'd had. I didn't want to dance at the club, so Amber had danced with all the others, Jake included. I'd watched them, wondering what was wrong with me, and why I was in such a sour mood.

It hadn't improved by the time we were on our way back to NYU on the subway. In fact, with Amber leaning against my shoulder sleepily, and Jake across the aisle staring out the windows as if he wasn't even part of our group, and Daniel and Seb both fawning over Jay, it got worse. My need to do *something* became unbearable.

"We're getting out at Spring Street," I announced, just before we arrived at that stop.

"What for?" asked Daniel.

"I don't want to walk," Jay complained. "It's too cold."

"Me neither," said Amber. "It's too late, Andy."

"I could go for some breakfast," said Seb hopefully, because there were several all-night diners near the Spring Street station.

Jake just stood up and stuffed his hands in his pockets as if ready to go. He gave me a questioning look, but said nothing.

"We're not walking," I told them. "We'll catch the next train. Come on."

The subway pulled into the Spring Street station and, without waiting to see if anyone else was actually going to follow me, I stepped onto the platform.

There was no one around at this time of night, and the trains ran less frequently, coming every twenty minutes. I paced back and forth, running the idea through my head, making sure of what I intended to do and trying to judge my own sobriety. I didn't feel drunk, only filled with that awful restless feeling that badly needed an outlet.

When the train pulled out, I found all my friends standing on the platform watching me.

"So what are we doing here?" Daniel asked. He was another pre-law student and not a guy to keep his mouth shut.

"A dare," I said abruptly. "I'm going to subway surf to Washington Square. My man Jake here won a bet the other day and told me to come up with a dare. So this is it. This acceptable to you, Jake?"

Jake was standing a bit apart to my left, so I was able to turn away from the group and give him a look. It was a look that said, *Play along, Jake. Let's get them good.* It was a look that, I hoped, promised excitement and thrills. Now that I'd decided what to do, manic energy flooded through me, making me feel amazing, making me feel invincible. There were protests from Amber and Jay, but I wasn't listening.

Jake blinked at me, his jaw going firm and stubborn. "Give us a second, guys," he said lightly. He gripped my elbow and pulled me down the platform and around the corner to the escalators.

When we were out of sight of our friends, and presumably out of earshot, Jake turned to me, his expression worried. "What do you think you're doing, Andy? This is way too dangerous."

"It isn't," I insisted. "Spring Street to Washington Park is only one stop. I'll be fine."

"You can't know that! People have died subway surfing. It's not a good stunt, it's just stupid." He folded his arms over his chest, looking extremely serious.

"Come on!" I scoffed. "Since when are you so chicken? Besides, you're not doing it, I am. I just need you to play it up. You know the script."

"No. You've been drinking, it's not safe. And it's too late. You're tired, we're all tired. This isn't the right time. Plus this isn't like other stunts we've done, where you had it planned out and we practiced. This is just . . . I mean, what the hell, Andy? You want to hang on the outside of a moving subway train? You could hit an obstruction in the tunnels, or lose your grip and fall. No, it's not cool. Really not cool, man."

Jake's negativity was seriously harshing my buzz. I thought he'd be down with this, excited even.

"I'm sorry, is it too late for you?" I said mockingly. "What, were you wanting to get back to the dorm so you could go over to Kevin's?"

Jake physically took a step back, looking at me like I was crazy. "What are you talking about? I'm not . . . Why would I go over to Kevin's at this time of night?"

I shut my mouth. *Damn it, why did I say that?* It had nothing to do with anything.

Instead of arguing with him further, I stood there and made myself breathe, made myself think through the stunt, try to see it from his perspective. I didn't feel drunk or tired. I was fine, more than jacked up enough for a challenge. And it wasn't as spur of the moment as he thought.

I didn't *want* to explain my thoughts about the stunt to Jake. I wanted him to be impressed, as impressed as everyone else would be, and maybe a little scared for me too. But that wasn't going to work. Jake wasn't going to go along with it if I didn't give him some reassurances. And while he couldn't physically stop me, it would fall flat if he didn't play along. And I wasn't sure I was ready to piss him off that badly.

I sighed. "Okay. I have thought it through. I've been following reports of subway surfing pretty much since we got here. I figured I might want to try it one day. You know me, bro. I've always got a dozen ideas for stunts up my sleeve."

He looked at me warily. "Go on."

"I found a forum where people talk about doing it. This stretch here, from Spring Street to Washington Square, is a safe zone. Lots of people have done it. It's a straight shot, not a lot of curves and no obstacles. I even saw a video of a guy doing it. It's not really that dangerous."

He made a frustrated face and ruffled his hair with one hand. "But things change. What if they're doing construction or something, and there are new obstacles? Or you could fall."

"Dude, how inept do you think I am? I won't fall. Come on! This is way less dangerous than other stuff we've done."

"Maybe," he conceded. "But I'm not as stupid as I used to be."

"Well I am," I said firmly.

I knew it would make him laugh, and it did. He chuckled and still looked at me like I was crazy, but I could see he'd softened. He was going to give in.

"Come on," I urged. "I'm not drunk at all. Swear to God. And this is perfect timing. It's late enough that there'll be few witnesses and both platforms will be empty. And we have some people with us to see it and freak out. What do you say? Please?" I pouted out my lip and gave him puppy-dog eyes.

With a show of reluctance, he sighed. "Fine. I still don't like it."

"Great! I need my wingman. Let's scare the crap out of them. You in?"

"Yeah. You get hurt, and I'll kill you."

"Understood, bro. Understood."

We did scare the crap out of them. Jake played up the danger, talking about warning notices from the New York City Transit Authority and the various ways it could go bad. I acted a little bit drunk—didn't want to overdo it. Amber and the others got emotionally invested, just as they should. Amber wanted the guys to "stop me" and Daniel said no, we should let Darwin's Law play out. Asshat. But everyone was wide-awake now.

At last the next train arrived and Jake got the group onboard. As soon as the doors closed and the train started to move, I jumped onto the outside of a door, gripping the sides the way I'd seen guys do on videos. The train rumbled and shook beneath me, giving me a rush as it went faster and faster. Jake stood on the other side of the door, palms pressed to the glass, his eyes locked on mine.

Don't you fucking fall, his eyes said.

I stuck my tongue out at him.

Like a roller coaster ride, it was over before I had time to really enjoy it. The train pulled into the Washington Square station, slowing, and I jumped onto the platform. As I thundered up the escalator, taking the steps three at a time, I heard a conductor or driver, some older guy, shouting angrily at me from down below. But he didn't chase me. I waited for my group outside the station. I received my accolades. Amber refused to speak to me.

We parted company with the last of our friends at the dorm, and Jake and I entered our room. He shut the door with finality as I turned on the light. Something about the sound of the closing door—not quite a slam, but close—made me turn to look at him. His face was stark and drawn. All the bravado and good humor he'd shown during the stunt was gone. And I realized it had all been a lie—Jake, the perfect wingman, had faked it.

Before I could say anything, he stepped up to me and grabbed me in a hug. It was a crushing hug that was nearly violent, his arms going around me, pinning my own arms down. I could hardly breathe—I'd had no idea he was that strong. But I didn't try to shake him off.

"Fuck, are you trying to break my ribs?" I gasped.

"Never again," he said in a hollow voice. "Not like that. You *tell* me first. We discuss it well beforehand. And nothing like that, where we have no control and . . ." His words broke off like he didn't know what he meant to say, all the conditions he meant to list. But I got the point.

"Yeah. Okay."

"Swear?"

"It's fine, Jake. I told you it wasn't really dangerous."

He shook his head, but he released me. A few minutes later he was in bed, his back to the room. I turned out the lights, slipped off my jeans and sweater, and got into my own bed in a T-shirt and briefs, not caring enough to brush my teeth or change my clothes.

I lay there for a while, thoughts churning in my head.

It hadn't *really* been dangerous. Not any more dangerous and probably less so than other stunts I'd done, like the school roof parkour. But I'd decided to do it last minute and sprung it on Jake. And I'd pushed him to go along with it. And I *had* drunk alcohol at the club, even if I hadn't felt drunk.

I was uneasy, a little guilty. I'd been compelled to do it, *needed* to. Why? What drove me to show off like that? Amber? No. She hated my stunts worse than anything. We always had a huge fight afterward, something I knew I'd be subjected to in the next few days.

Why, then, did I feel the need to do it?

I thought of the way Jake had hugged me just now, grateful that I was alive, that I was okay. Was I really so jealous of Kevin that I had to prove Jake was still my best friend? Or was I trying to punish him?

Whatever. It was way too much introspection for a Saturday night. Everything was fine. It was just a stunt. There was no point in getting hung up about it. I'd just be cool for a few months, and next time, I'd make sure Jake was in on the plans so he wouldn't freak.

I smiled to myself in the dark. There was always a next time.

August 2017
Jake

It was our last two weeks together at the cottage, and all bets were off. We weren't pretending anymore. Well, there were things I still wasn't saying, couldn't say. We didn't discuss our feelings, God forbid.

But there was no more pretending we didn't want each other all the time.

We feasted on sex like people about to go on a starvation diet. The jet skis languished unused at the dock.

The next big step came two days after Andy fucked me for the first time. I loved it, loved that it was *Andy* taking over my body like that, and we did it in every conceivable position. True to his nature, nothing about it put him off or made him hesitate in the least. He was all gung ho. He wanted to know how it felt, from this angle and that. When he figured out the prostate thing, he became merciless in driving me to orgasm, usually with my hand flying over myself as he pounded me hard, though one memorable time he did the honors while taking me from behind.

After the fifth time, though, I had to beg off for a day or so. I was getting too sore to bottom, as badly as I wanted to.

That Monday was all blue skies and a heaven-sent breeze that blew away the humidity on the shoreline. After breakfast, we played football out on the cottage's back lawn. I was a little worried about hurting the baby-new skin on our palms with hard football passes, but Andy insisted we could throw the ball lightly, and so we did.

We passed the ball and ran and generally burnt off steam. And then I tackled him onto the grass, facefirst.

I refused to let him up, wanting to mess with him. Though Andy was a little taller than me, I was at least as strong. I held him down, spreading out over his back, pinning his wrists and trapping his calves under mine.

"Get off, you ox!" Andy sputtered.

"Not until you say 'Jake Masterson is the best-looking, most intelligent human being I know.'"

Andy laughed, but it was a choked sound with me pressing on his back. "You douche."

"Say it. Say—"

"Jake Masterson is a disgusting human being."

"Um, yeah, not really close." I bounced a little on his back, making his breath huff out like a deranged Santa Claus. *Huh, huh, huh.* "Say it."

"No." He sounded breathless, but not distressed. I bounced on him a little again, hoping to induce him to cooperate.

"Say 'Jake Masterson has the biggest dick I've ever seen, and he really knows how to use it.'"

Andy tried to laugh again. He thumped his head on the grass. "You know I could throw you off if I wanted to."

"Yeah? Let's see it," I dared him, tightening my hold.

"Don't want to." He pressed his ass up seductively into my groin.

The game went from funny to achingly sexy in a heartbeat. I got hard so fast, the grass spun a little. As if it turned him on to feel me swell against him, Andy groaned and pushed up again. "Do me. I want you to."

"Now?" I asked dubiously. It wasn't that Andy and I had a timetable for sex. We'd pretty much done it any time of the day and everywhere inside the cottage. But for the past few days, Andy had talked about me fucking him but had never seemed that serious about it. And suddenly he was ready at ten in the morning?

"Yeah, now," he said, his voice gravelly. "Get off me."

"Get off you so we can get off? Seems a little contradictory," I quipped. But I ground my hardness into his plump ass cheek and licked his neck. When Andy murmured a desperate noise, I pinned him down harder. "Say it."

"Jake Masterson has the biggest dick in the world, and if he doesn't get up right now and fuck me with it, we'll both be exceedingly sorry!" he declared, loudly.

I chuckled, got up, and helped him to his feet.

In his bedroom, Andy didn't hesitate to strip his clothes or boss me around. "Get on your back. I want to lower myself onto that flagpole of yours."

"We need to open you up first," I argued, nevertheless arranging myself, naked, on the bed, sitting with my back against the headboard where I figured Andy could get a good grip.

"Then do it." He crawled onto the bed, lube in hand, and straddled me, staying up on his knees.

I took the lube and coated my fingers. They felt cold against the intense heat of his body. God, he was so warm. I circled behind his balls and around his hole, teasing, wanting to make this good for him.

He didn't rush me, just braced his hands on my shoulders, on either side of my neck, and let me work. His gaze was locked on mine, intent, and some part of him turned inward too, as if concentrating on the sensation. We only broke eye contact when I had to look down to put more lube on my fingers, and then to put the condom on.

Like the fearless creature that he was, Andy sank down on me slowly, with widened eyes, black with a thin rim of blue, and with zero hesitation. I bit my lip hard, using pain to back off the pleasure, and wondered how I was supposed to ever move on from this, from having Andy naked and earthy and carnal in my hands, running full tilt at life, at sex, at me.

I held his hips to support him as he began to move up and down. He had narrow hips, a very long waist, and a tiny mound of a belly, incongruous when the rest of him was still so lean. His thighs were muscled and strong, tensing and flexing as he rose.

The tightness began to ease, and he began to go faster. I clenched my jaw against the waves of pleasure that wanted to spiral up too soon. I gripped his hips harder, needing to slow him down. He stopped utterly then, resting on my thighs. He leaned forward, wrapping his arms around my neck, and kissed me. And kissed. And kissed.

It was so sweet, to pause on the knife's edge of pleasure and just rock there, minutely, keeping the fire stoked. My eyes were closed, and I rubbed my hands over his back, loving that I could touch him this way now. I massaged him low, where only a thin wall of muscle separated my hands from my dick, buried deep inside him. Emotion rose up, and I thought I might lose it. I swallowed down every feeling, hiding them in a locked box inside my heart. This was not the time. Maybe there never would be a time, but right now, I had to make this good. *Sexy* good.

He finally broke off kissing me to say, "It doesn't hurt."

"Good."

"Definitely feels weird though, being on the receiving end."

I raised an eyebrow and held his hips to keep them still as I ground up into him. The slight teasing motion I achieved sent delight echoing through my shaft and balls. I licked my lips and gave him what I hoped was a sexy, half-lidded stare.

"Lean back," I told him. "Put your hands by my knees. Let's see if I can find your prostate."

He did as I asked, spreading his torso back over my thighs. I raised his hips up and thrust into him. I was so hard there was no bend in my dick at all, despite the weird angle. He hissed in a breath when I stuck him deep.

"That it?" I asked.

He nodded eagerly. "God *damn*. What the hell is that? Do it again."

I didn't take his question literally. He knew what a prostate was, it was just his first time feeling it. I supported his hips a few inches above me and began to seriously pound up into him. He threw his head back and groaned, kept groaning in harsh, staccato bursts every time I nailed him. The sounds he made, the sight of him stretched out like that, were almost better, *more*, than the sensation of his tight, hot channel. Sweat slicked me as I worked, giving him everything I had. I was determined not to stop and not to rest. His dick was stiff as steel as it bounced on his stomach, and a line of clear pre-come stretched with every bounce. He had to be close.

I was close. I was almost beyond thought.

"Touch yourself," I gasped. "Almost there." I had to see him come before I did.

But he just raised his head to look at me. "Don't need to. D-don't stop. Jake!" His lips trembled and his face was flushed red. His expression was tense, one I'd seen a dozen times—it was the face he had when he came.

I doubled my efforts in an inspired burst, pounding up into him for one second, two . . .

"Oh God." His head dropped back again. His dick began to release come onto his belly in a constant stream, not in pulses like a normal orgasm, but more like cream slowly pouring out of a cup.

My hands clenched, and I curled forward as my own orgasm ripped through me, hot and sweet and intense as anything I'd ever felt in my life.

Later, when we were rearranged, the condom had been disposed of, and my heart had come down from Mach 5, I whistled. "That was the first time I've ever seen that. Someone coming hands-free."

"Yeah. Weird, right?" He was lying on his back, one hand behind his head on the pillow. The other stroked my forearm lightly. "Never happened to me before."

"Not unheard of, but pretty rare, yeah."

"Once you started hitting my prostate I could feel something building inside me. It wasn't exactly like a regular orgasm, but it was super intense. Longer and more . . . aching, maybe?"

"Hmmm. So you liked it, then? Being fucked, I mean?"

He rolled onto his side and threw his arm over my chest, limp as a noodle. "Yeah. Your magic dick made a bottom out of me."

I smirked. "Idiot."

He closed his eyes and appeared to go to sleep immediately.

I lay there, my fingertips grazing his arm. I wanted to ask him: *So what does that mean for your future? Will you have your girlfriends or wife peg you? Will you someday find another male lover to fuck around with now and then when you're married? Or could you take or leave it? Would you be fine never repeating the experience again?*

I wanted to ask him those things, but I wouldn't. Not later, when he was awake. Not ever.

Andy was the brave one. Not me.

Chapter
EIGHTEEN

JAKE

Inevitably, Friday the eighteenth arrived, our last day at the lake. The dawn came, despite me silently begging for it not to. I had maybe slept three hours that night, and I lay in bed in Andy's room, watching the sky go from black to a dim purple to pink at the horizon. Time wasn't on our side.

I became too filled with nervous energy to lie still, so I got up and showered, leaving Andy to sleep.

As I put on the coffee, Andy appeared. He came dragging into the kitchen in his PJ bottoms, looking about as uneasy as I felt.

"Morning, Sleeping Beauty," I said. "Nice hair you got going on there." A tuft of Andy's blond hair was sticking straight up in back.

He gave me a half-hearted glare and poured himself a cup of coffee. We stood at the sink looking out the window at the sound together.

"Had a text from my dad last night," he said. "He has a client meeting at three, so he expects to be here after five o'clock."

I felt a trace of relief at that. At least we had most of the day. "Okay."

He leaned against me, putting his head on my shoulder, which was quite a trick since he was taller than me. I put my arm around his back and squeezed. We stood there for about five minutes, just looking out at the sea. I'd opened the window to get some fresh air, and the sound of the water lapping the shore was loud, mesmerizing.

I was going to have a thing about the ocean forever now, wasn't I?

After a while, Andy gently pulled away and shuffled off to take a shower.

We had cereal for breakfast, surfed the web for a while on our respective laptops, sitting together at the kitchen table, then finished up our packing. Andy was antsy, and so was I, so we went for a run. Time was being so weird. It was alternatively racing by and lagging torturously. By the time we got back from our run it was only 11 a.m., too early for lunch.

We drank bottled water in the kitchen, sweaty in our running clothes. Andy looked at me and I looked at him. And it was like we hadn't just run at all. All that rubber-band tension and worry and stress in my chest was back in a heartbeat.

We were separating today. And though we'd talked about FaceTime and meeting up over Christmas/Hanukkah in Boston, it wouldn't be the same. Would Andy even want me once he was at Harvard with access to hundreds of women? He'd probably be in another relationship by October.

It fucking *hurt*.

In a blink, Andy tossed his bottle in the sink and reached out for me. We grabbed on to each other like we were both lost at sea. We kissed and clutched each other's sweaty back, pressing tight. Instantly, I wanted him. Right then and preferably for the rest of the day. We—

"Andrew!" The voice broke through my haze like a rifle shot.

Andy jerked away. His dad stood in the doorway to the living room, a grocery bag in his arms. His expression was shocked. His skin slowly darkened to a mottled red.

I glanced at Andy. He was frozen, staring at his dad in disbelief. "H-hey, Dad," he managed.

"What the hell are you doing?" Mr. Tyler asked this with absolute surprise and horror, as if he were saying *What the hell are these psychotic clowns doing in my kitchen?*

Fuck. This was bad. This was really bad. I held my tongue, waiting to see how Andy was going to respond.

I saw the casual, life-of-the-party mask go up over Andy's face. That *Aren't I just a rascal?* look. It made me feel a little ill. "We were just goofing off. What did you bring?"

Andy took a step toward his dad, eyeing the bag he was carrying.

His dad wasn't buying it. "Goofing off? Andrew, are you . . . are you *gay?*"

The question was blunt and harsh, and Andy flinched. "No! I . . ." He looked at me, as if asking for help. I stared back at him wordlessly.

Please don't do this, I thought. But I could already tell he'd go to the wall to play it off as nothing.

Andy looked back at his dad. "I'm not gay. It's just . . . we were alone up here together all summer, and . . ." He shrugged. "It's not a big deal. My generation isn't as hung up on labels."

Mr. Tyler's lips thinned, and he blinked twice. He made a noise of exasperation and, as if realizing he was still holding the bag, he stepped to the kitchen table and put it down. He turned to look me over, his eyes angry, then shifted his gaze back to Andy. He was practically bristling. Andy crossed his arms over his chest and looked at the fridge.

"Well, it's a big deal to me!" his dad said, incensed. "Something like this . . . If you start down this path, it could ruin your entire future!"

Andy rolled his eyes. "How? It's not like we're on the front page of a tabloid. There are no paparazzi here."

"But the two of you . . .! We're going to discuss this. Are you and Jake a . . . a couple? How long have you been hiding this from me? And what about Amber? Was that all a lie, all those girls?"

"No!" Andy said fiercely. "I told you, I'm *not gay*. Two guys can fool around without it meaning they're gay. There's such a thing as bisexuality. Or experimenting. Or even expediency. For Christ's sake."

My face burned. Terrific. Within a few seconds I'd been reduced from a possible bisexual hookup to an experiment to an expedient hot orifice. I'd had enough. And then I realized I should leave father and son alone to talk anyway. I finally found the will to move.

"Excuse me," I said, hot emotion choking me. Anger. Hurt. I walked to the back door.

"Jake," Andy said, regret in his voice.

"Jake Masterson, this conversation is not over!" said Mr. Tyler.

Why the fuck did he want me there? Was he planning to grill me too? Maybe he felt like he had the right since he'd been around me since I was in middle school. But he didn't. He wasn't paying my way, like he was Andy. Nothing was going to keep me in that room to hear Andy shred us until nothing remained but a dirty smear of shame.

"You're not my father!" I gritted out between clenched teeth, then I banged out the back door and took off across the lawn.

ANDY

My dad paced the kitchen, looking shocked and disgusted. Jake had taken off, visibly upset. Not that I blamed him. It was my fault. I was an idiot for making out in the kitchen when I knew my dad would be driving down today.

"I thought you said you wouldn't be here before five," I said.

My dad shot me an accusing glare. "My afternoon appointment canceled. Am I to understand that you would have deliberately hidden this from me if I hadn't walked in on it?"

I shrugged. "It's not the sort of thing you share with your parents. You don't discuss your sex life with me, and thank God for that."

"Don't be smart! This is just another one of your stupid stunts, isn't it?"

"What?" I said in surprise. "It's not a stunt."

But I could tell he wasn't listening. He seemed furious, as furious as I'd ever seen him. His voice shook as he spoke. "I've never said this to you, Andrew, but for a long time now I've been afraid there was something wrong with you, some kind of crossed wires in that head of yours that makes you do these stupid, self-destructive things."

I froze, blinking hard. My dad truly thought that?

"It's as though ninety-five percent of you has your head on straight, works hard, and approaches the future in a serious manner. And then there's this wild thread that just delights in trying to smash everything you've ever accomplished into a million pieces!"

"That's not true! I work my ass off and always have. As for the private moment you happened to walk in on, it was *private*. Guys my age fool around and drink and act out sometimes. I'm way more responsible than most of the people I know. Do you expect me to behave like an old man?"

My dad went on as if I hadn't spoken. "I hoped as you got older and started law school, moved away from . . . from Jake and his influence, you'd mature out of it. Or simply wouldn't have time for it anymore. But things have gotten worse! First you about blow your hands off, and now you're screwing around with a boy? Honestly, Andrew, sometimes I worry for your sanity." My dad's face was both angry and bewildered, like he was really at his wits' end.

That was really what he thought of me? He worried for my *sanity*? Shame and anger soured my stomach.

I didn't feel capable of saying anything that he would listen to, or that wouldn't be a rant and a very bad idea. So I went to the fridge and got out a pitcher of iced tea Emily had left. I poured two glasses, put them on the table, and sat down in a chair. After a moment, my dad sat down and picked up his glass. His mouth was set in a firm line.

Looking at him, I had a flash of realization—I was so much like him. It was a déjà vu type of feeling. Was that what my face looked like when I was angry? Did I appear that unhappy all the time? Would I when I was his age?

We sat there silently for a moment. I plucked up and rejected words like I was sorting stones on the shore. Neither of my parents were shouters. They were both intelligent enough that they could gut you—or each other—without the necessity of raising their voices. If I was going to get anywhere with my father, I had to use cold logic.

Finally, I began in a reasonable voice, "I'm sorry you were shocked. No, I'm not gay. I suppose I'm bisexual, technically, but it's been more opportunistic than anything."

"Have the two of you been fooling around since . . . all those nights he stayed at our house?"

"No," I said firmly but coolly. "It just happened this summer. It's not serious."

I felt guilty for saying it, and I was glad Jake wasn't here to hear the words. It wasn't exactly true, but what Jake and I had was none of my dad's business. And we were separating soon anyway. What was the point in freaking out my father?

He looked at me then. He still appeared angry, but there was a spark of hope in his eyes, as if he *wanted* me to convince him.

"As I said, it's not like it was in your day. Sex is just sex. There's not the stigma attached to it that there would have been for you."

My dad shook his head tersely. "You may believe that, but, as usual, you're not thinking about consequences. This is just like holding those lit firecrackers. You refuse to see the danger. What if someone finds out about you and Jake? Is that something you want your future employers to know? Do you want them to think you're gay or bisexual? You do realize that with the new administration, conservatism is on the rise. And what about Amber? Or the woman you'll eventually marry? I'm assuming when you say this thing with Jake is 'just sex,' you do intend to continue having relationships with women?"

"Of course," I said tightly.

"And how will your future wife feel about this, knowing you're A-okay with having sex with a man? Will she be able to feel secure in you then? Hell, what if Jake thinks this is more serious than it is and gets his feelings hurt? For God's sake, Andrew, why can't you think things through!"

My dad's tone wasn't harsh so much as it was logical, adamant, and cajoling, as if pleading with me to see reason. But it was worse that way—disappointment instead of anger. The words socked me in the gut and made me feel about an inch tall.

And I had to wonder if he was right. Whenever my dad talked about the future, I could see it all laid out in front of me in black and white. When I saw it like that, I wanted to do the right thing, the safe thing. I really did. What *about* my employers? Things had been looser with gay marriage and all that, but he was right that there was a strong swing back the other way. My mom had warned me that the legal field was still a conservative one. And what *would* my someday wife think? Would I have to tell her?

But even the idea of "my wife" echoed, strange and incomprehensible, in my head. I found it hard to care about some future, hypothetical person when Jake was in my life right now. Only he wasn't really. We both had our paths laid out, and they weren't together. The cottage had been like an island, an escape from the real world. But we couldn't ignore the real world forever.

My dad's reaction was a harsh wake-up call. He wasn't a stupid man. He was usually right. I wasn't stupid either. I'd always known continuing things with Jake wasn't consistent with my plans. *Was* there a crazy part of my brain that just wanted to destroy everything? Had I destroyed me and Jake? The thought was unbearable.

"I'm sorry you feel that way about it," I said in a soft voice. I stood up, unable to take the disillusioned look on my dad's face any longer.

"Andrew—"

"I don't think it would be productive to continue the conversation right now."

I went out the back door, closing it quietly behind me to show that I was in control of myself.

Jake

Andy found me sitting on a log at the top of the beach. It was a private spot that was hidden from the cottage by trees. I didn't want his dad to be able to see me, God knew why. It wasn't like Mr. Tyler would have come after me. Maybe I was ashamed. Not about what Andy and I had done, but for the way Andy made me feel about what we had done.

Andy stopped when he came around the trees and saw me. He hesitated. I didn't look at him, my gaze fixed on the water.

"I'm really sorry about that," he said at last.

I didn't answer. I was so hurt and angry, it felt like a nest of hornets had taken up residence in my chest and they were stinging me internally. I didn't trust myself to speak. I wrapped my arms around myself, despite it being a hot day, and leaned forward, staring at nothing.

"Don't worry about it," Andy said. "There's nothing he can say or do to you. It's the end of the summer anyway. As for me, he'll get over it."

"Sure." My voice was tight. "I suppose today was going to be depressing anyway, so why not make it a complete clusterfuck?"

As if those words had somehow encouraged him—Andy always was a contrary bastard—he came over and sat down on the log beside me, not close enough to brush shoulders, but almost.

We sat there for a while, not saying anything. What was there to say? We'd already talked about keeping in touch, made vague remarks about FaceTime and all of that. We'd cautiously talked around it for days, saying things like *I'll miss this* after sex and even, once, Andy had said, "God, I'll miss you," after I'd made a stupid pun about the butter. We'd been best friends forever, lived together for the past four years, so obviously we'd miss each other. The words were safe to say, safe to pin on friendship.

There was one thing we'd never talked about, though. And I hadn't intended to, ever. But sitting there on the shore, with the sting of Andy's words, saying that touching me had meant nothing, like a fresh wound in my chest, I suddenly had to say it. Because I knew this was the end—not just of the summer but probably of everything. And Andy deserved to know why. And I deserved to get it off my chest. And maybe I just didn't give a shit anymore.

"The thing is," I began, my voice rough, "once I get to California, I'm going to need some space. A few months at least. Maybe longer."

"Space?" Andy sounded confused.

It felt like ripping out my guts to say it. "Time to think about things, get my head together without—with no contact. Between us."

That sank in, the air heavy as lead.

"Are you pissed off? About what I said to my dad? I admit, I kinda panicked there. I didn't—"

"That's not it," I cut in, unable to bear his excuses. I took a deep breath. "Okay. So I didn't tell you about Kevin, or about me figuring out I was bisexual, because I thought if you knew, you'd think maybe your best friend had been in love with you all these years." A chill went up my spine. I couldn't believe I was saying the words. "And I didn't want you to think that. Even though . . . you would have been right. Especially because you would have been right."

I hugged my knees and squeezed them. Next to me, Andy was quiet.

"I should never have agreed to have sex with you," I continued. "I know it meant nothing to you. And I thought, at first, that it could mean nothing to me too. But that was ridiculous." I laughed bitterly. "I'd moved on emotionally, right? The past few years. Then you sucked me back in again. Literally. Good job there, bro."

I risked a glance at Andy, because I had to. He was looking at me, his eyes wounded and his expression stark. "Jake . . . I. Are you saying . . . Why didn't you tell me?"

I shrugged, looking away again. *He really doesn't know.* "There was no point. I'm only telling you this now because I'm going to need some time to get my shit together, to get into my new job and all of that without being . . . being distracted with a bunch of drama. We've been friends forever, and I'm not saying we can't continue to be. Just . . . not for a while. We said it would be a clean break when we left here. I need time to make that stick. And that's it."

"Jake." Andy's voice was disbelieving, but there was anguish in there. "I'm sorry. You know I . . . *Christ.* You know I . . . love you too."

In the hesitation, I heard what he didn't say: *like a brother.* Well, not exactly like a brother, apparently. Because that would be gross. But close enough.

"It's not your fault." My fingers dug into the sand to keep from reaching for him. "It's all on me. Always has been. It is what it is."

I got up and left him there, walking back toward the house.

Pushing inside the back door, I didn't look at Mr. Tyler or speak to him. I went to my room, got my bags, took them out to the car, and sat in the back seat, waiting to be driven home.

Dare
#5

Chapter
NINETEEN

ANDY

Harvard had a spectacular campus and law school. I knew that ahead of time, of course, from the trips my dad and I had taken to visit it. I clearly remembered the thrill of those glimpses of a grown-up, serious life. I could remember being *so damn impressed* and wanting it *so badly*. I remembered worrying that I wouldn't be good enough to earn a spot.

My dad had drilled it into me how difficult it was to get in, especially with all the diversity initiatives. I had to have a perfect record to have a prayer. I'd worked hard to get straight As. I'd joined clubs and did some volunteering because my dad thought it would look good on my résumé. And my mom had gotten me letters of recommendation from two of the top lawyers in Boston. Still, I was incredibly fortunate to be accepted. Arriving there to begin law school should have been a dream come true—satisfying, exciting.

It wasn't. It felt surreal, like I was a stunt double in someone else's life. I expected the director to show up at any moment and call a wrap and let me off duty to go back to the cottage. To go back to Jake.

I tried to shake it off. It was pathetic and stupid; I knew that. I'd worked so hard for this. I promised myself I'd give it my best shot. I had to.

That last day at the cottage had been such a god-awful mess. First my dad catching me and Jake making out—he hadn't told my mom, said we would "put it aside," but he still wasn't over it. The worst part, though, was that my time with Jake had ended all wrong. Jake and I should have parted ways with a final hug, sincere *I'll miss you*s, and a plan for keeping in touch. Instead, I'd hurt his feelings in front of my dad, Jake had admitted he'd been in love with me for years, and he'd told me he didn't want to talk to me—at least, not anytime soon. Through it all, I'd been like a deer in headlights, not knowing how to react, what to say.

Jake has been in love with me for years?

God, I knew my wingman was a good actor, but I'd never had a clue. Looking back now, I could sort of see it. He'd hid it well, and we'd double-dated through a lot of high school. Jake had had girlfriends, a few fairly serious, I'd thought. But if I remembered how close we were, how touchy-feely we were for guys, the occasional jealousy he showed toward chicks, then yeah, I could see it.

I'd definitely felt him pulling away from me during college, but there'd always been an excuse—we'd been busy, had classes, work, or finals. I'd felt us growing apart and tried to combat it, talking him into going out for pizza together or going to shoot some ball or take a run.

Then I'd completely lost my mind and talked him into having sex, wanting to try it out, needing to *know*. Yeah, that had been smart. Now I didn't even have my best friend.

Maybe my dad was right. Maybe I was self-destructive. Maybe my wires were crossed in some vital way.

It hurt. I walked around Harvard with an invisible knife in my gut. I couldn't stop obsessing over what I should have done, or said, to reach a different outcome. What if this had happened? What if that? I should never have suggested Jake and I get each other off. Conversely, I should have refused to let him go.

But this wasn't the end of *The Graduate*, where Dustin Hoffman walked into the back of the church and stole the bride. They didn't have to show you what happened next in a movie. But what happened next was really fucking important in real life.

If Jake's head had gotten screwed up during our summer at the lake, mine had too. I'd given in to curiosity and learned that, yes, I was bisexual. It turned out I loved having sex with a guy—or at least, with Jake. I loved how raw and real it was with him, no bullshit, no pretense, no hearts and flowers, just bodies and closeness and orgasms. I loved how every time I wanted it, he wanted it too. All I had to do was look at him a certain way and he was in the mood. I'd never experienced that with anyone I'd dated, never been so in-tune at a cellular level.

I also loved how easy it was to be with Jake every minute of the day, how having sex only opened up even more time and more ways for us to be together. I couldn't get enough of holding him, kissing him. With every girlfriend I'd ever had, I'd wanted to be with them sometimes, but I'd crave time apart too, time to myself, or guy time. Time with Jake was like a closed circuit. Being with him was so easy and natural and fun, it just made me want to be with him more.

But it was one thing to be that way with Jake at the cottage. It wasn't realistic to drag it into real life, not least because we both had things we wanted to do, *had* to do, in opposite corners of the world. And that wasn't even the biggest problem. As much as I loved being with Jake, when I tried to project us down the road with him in the role of *boyfriend, husband, co-parent*, I just . . . couldn't. That was not my life, the life I'd planned for years. My future included the whole picket-fence-wife-kids-dog package. Someday, when I was ready to settle down, it would be with a woman. Even in my weakest moments, when I held my phone in bed and fucking *ached* to call him, I knew I had to be strong. There was no future in it. Jake had been right. It was best to cut it off, make a clean break, feel the pain now, get over it, and then move on. And maybe when it didn't hurt so damn much, we could be friends again.

My classes started. I was taking Corporate Transactions, Antitrust Law, Boards of Directors and Corporate Governance, and Business Strategy for Lawyers. I'd known in advance it wouldn't be very exciting stuff this first semester. Or ever. My classes were all geared toward my ultimate aim—corporate law. But even here, even at Harvard Law School, a bastion of secure and conservative career paths, I couldn't help but envy the students who were actually excited about their classes.

I'd hear them talking in the cafeteria or in the lounge at Hastings, my residence.

"No, the *Camarena* case set precedent. You can't force extradite someone from Mexico, not even for a capital crime!"

"But Rodriguez was only seventeen, and he was brought back by a relative. Therefore—"

Criminal law students. Social justice advocates. There were so many incredibly bright and passionate students around me. They were going to change the world, or at least contribute something meaningful. They were totally engaged. And I was . . .

I was going to draw up contracts for corporate mergers, and pen terms and conditions that protected businesses from liability no matter how shitty their products were. I was as far from inspired as I could get.

You can do other work in law if you want, just do it pro bono, like you mother does. I could hear my dad's voice in my head. *Once you're established, you'll have time to take cases on the side. But you have to secure your bread and butter first. That's only smart.*

It had always made sense to me. Because, fuck, I didn't want to struggle for money, to not be able to provide good health care or schools for my family. I didn't want to retire on plan Z. I wanted the life my parents had. Security. Respect. Success. And I figured I'd still be able to do what I wanted some of the time, so where was the problem?

Only now that law school had started, I could see the problem clearly. Or maybe it was the state my head was in after Jake. Maybe at another time, I could have powered through my boring classes. But I felt so awful and, frankly, depressed, that I had no reserves of patience, no energy left to power through anything.

The truth was: corporate law was dry and dull and tedious as fuck. And if this was going to be my primary job, I'd be stuck doing it the majority of my working hours for the rest of my life. Was that how I wanted to live? It was one thing to think about that in the abstract, from the perspective of a high schooler with big plans. It was another to actually do it day by day by boring day. And yeah, my mother did it. I *should* be able to do it. But maybe I was too selfish or too spoiled. I didn't want that life.

Maybe I didn't want any of it. Maybe the entire ten-year plan was shit. All I wanted was Jake. I missed Jake. Right then, at Harvard, it felt like I'd gotten on the wrong plane. It was like everyone else was in their seat, reading or chatting, content with where they were going.

And I was roaming the aisle, lost and going the wrong way at hundreds of miles per hour.

I kept telling myself it was temporary. I told myself I'd get over Jake, that I shouldn't act rashly. Too much was at stake. *Everything.* Everything was on the line.

If I just gave it a chance, maybe I could get engaged with my classes. The fault obviously lay with me. Two years from now, I might meet an amazing woman. Perhaps I'd enjoy putting on an expensive suit every day and going into a fancy high-rise office in downtown New York or Boston, having elegant lunches, and hashing out the fine print on contracts. I *could live that life.* For fuck's sake, it wasn't like it would be a hardship. Anyone should be so lucky to have a life like that!

So why was my gut twisted up in a stubborn knot that refused to relax? Why did it feel like my heart was bruised and bleeding and shriveling up incremental bit by incremental bit, every day that passed?

I watched my feet tromp over the smooth asphalt of the paths around the Harvard campus and wondered at how disconnected I felt from my own body, my own life.

I wondered how long it would take until I could get through an entire day without once wishing I was dead.

Chapter
TWENTY

Jake

Andy didn't call me, and I didn't call him.

Four weeks passed. Very soon after leaving the cottage, I started work at Neverware. I'd been so desperate for a distraction, I'd flown to San Jose on Sunday, two days after Andy's dad dropped me off at my house. By Tuesday, I was working a ten-hour day at Neverware. Talk about making your head spin.

The company was cool though. I got my own desk in an open office space with about a dozen others. I received my own stapler, pens, notepads, and Post-its from office supply. I got a desktop computer with two monitors.

I went through two days of training with the guy who was currently maintaining the code on the product database system I was taking over. He showed me all the modules and how they were structured and what they looked like on the user end and on the shipping and fulfillment end. He showed me a couple of case studies of how they'd added features and made adjustments for new clients who'd bought the database system. After that I was on my own with eighty bug reports in Java, two new clients coming on board, and a baseball-sized lump of terror in my gut.

But after the first two weeks, one hundred and three bugs successfully closed, a handle on new incoming ones, and a client meeting under my belt, I realized I really could do the job. Meanwhile, it was nice to go to lunch with Sierra, even if all she wanted to talk about was her upcoming wedding. And there was a group of about ten Neverware peeps who went out for drinks on Friday nights.

I was living with Sierra for the time being, sleeping on the sofa in her one-bedroom apartment. It'd been fun for the first few days and then not so much. As much as we got along as brother and sister, the quarters were too close, and I wasn't in the friendliest of moods. She'd decided that after she and Tom got back from their honeymoon, she was going to move into his condo in Palo Alto, and I could take over her apartment. I honestly didn't care one way or the other. About much of anything.

Outwardly, everything was good. But there was a black, empty space where my heart had once been. Being a contrary organ, it hurt a lot for something that had been removed. I would wake up three or four times a night on the uncomfortable couch and reach for Andy or imagine he was beside me, only to remember he wasn't there. I even missed the cottage and the sound. I gladly would have burned my hands again for another two weeks with Andy there.

It didn't take long for Sierra to get me to spill my guts. I told her everything. She fed me Chunky Monkey ice cream, promised me I'd meet the guy or girl of my dreams before I knew it, and threatened to get me involved in making favors for her wedding when I acted too mopey. So like the sad clown, I hid my pain.

It was a Friday night in mid-September when Andy called. It was late. Sierra's fiancé, Tom, was out of town, so she and I had gone out with work friends for drinks, eaten Chinese, and come home around nine. We were almost done watching a movie when my phone buzzed. I looked at it, saw Andy's name. I put the phone in the pocket of my sweatshirt, unanswered.

Sierra glanced over at me. "Is it him?"

I nodded, my gaze trained on the TV screen as if I actually gave a damn about the show. A moment later, my phone buzzed again. I had my volume turned on low, but you could hear the hum of the vibration setting. I didn't bother to look at it.

Sierra paused the movie. I could tell by the look on her face that she was going into full Big Sister mode.

"You should answer it," she said in a firm voice. "Jesus, it's nearly midnight here. It's like 3 a.m. in Massachusetts."

"So?" She was right, it was late there. But if he was calling me in a moment of middle-of-the-night weakness, that was a good reason not to answer. Still. I felt a trickle of worry.

"What if he's sorry?" she insisted. "What if he wants to get back together?"

I snorted. "We were never together in the first place, so kind of impossible to get *back* together."

"You *were* together over the summer," Sierra insisted. "At least hear what he has to say. What if his mom died or something?"

I glared at her. "Yeah, let's go with that hypothesis. What are you, Occam's insane aunt?"

The phone in my pocket, which had stopped buzzing during this conversation, buzzed again.

"Obviously it's important." She pushed my arm. "Answer it, Jake! You at least owe him that much."

I wasn't convinced Andy's idea of important and my idea of important were the same, or that I owed him this. I'd been doing a bang-up job resisting the urge to call him. I knew I'd be undoing weeks of work if I answered the phone—like an AA member having that one drink. But now she'd gotten me worried and, worse, *hopeful*.

With a sigh that could have leveled empires with its sheer attitude, I took the phone out of my pocket and walked toward the kitchen to take the call.

"Hey," I said as I walked to the sink. It seemed prudent to be next to a place where I could either puke or get hydrated. And I was also close to the oven, so I could stick my head in there if needed, another bonus.

"Jake?" Andy's voice was shaky. "You picked up!"

He sounded surprised. Desperate. And maybe . . . drunk? There was a lot of white noise in the background. For a moment I thought he was on a subway or something. Then I realized it was wind. He was outside in a heavy wind. Was he walking somewhere on campus? I hoped he wasn't driving if he was drunk.

"Hey, what's up, bro?" I asked. Somewhere in my head, a warning bell sounded, but what it was warning me about wasn't yet clear.

"I'm at Harvard," Andy said, his voice too loud.

"Yeah, I know that. Have you been drinking?"

"Yeah. Pretty drunk. Hey, you should see it from up here. 'He campus. It's fucking cold tonight. Yanno? But 's pretty with all the lights."

My heart stopped. I leaned against the sink to try to ground myself. His voice. I'd never heard Andy sound quite like that before. It sent a chill up my spine. He sounded like a ghost of himself, fragile, broken. "Andy, where are you?"

"Roof. At Hastings. 'S pretty far up. Way higher than Dunsbar. Steeper too. Hey, remember that stunt?"

"Yeah, Andy. I remember." My tongue felt thick in my mouth. Fucking hell. He was definitely drunk, and on a *roof*? "What are you doing up there? Is anyone with you?"

"Huh?"

"Is someone with you?" I said, louder in case he couldn't hear me over the wind. In my peripheral vision, I saw Sierra in the doorway.

He ignored my questions. His voice turned sad. "Miss you, Jake. Miss you so much. I don't want this. 'S whole thing. I'm so *stupid*. I'm here, and it's the best school ever. Right? Yanno? But I don't want it. I don't. Don't know what to do, Jake. I hurt. So much. I thought it would get better, like pulling off a Band-Aid. 'S what I thought."

"Yeah." I closed my eyes. *Oh God*. At his words, my own pain burst to life, as hot and harsh and deep as it ever had been.

"Hasn't gotten better." It was barely a whisper. "'M so sick of feeling weak and confused and . . . Fuck. Jake."

"I know. I know. Me too." My heart split open for him. I'd never heard him sound so low. He was scaring me. "But listen to me, Andy. What are you doing on the roof, man? Huh? You said it was cold. Don't you think you should go inside and get warm? Then we can talk some more."

I looked up to see Sierra watching me anxiously, her arms crossed. I shook my head at her. *It's not okay.*

And it wasn't. Because I knew Andy. And I knew, didn't I, that when Andy was stressed or upset about something, that was when he was at his craziest. In the past, I'd been there, been able to keep him from doing anything too radical. I wasn't there now.

"Andy?" I repeated, when he didn't answer.

"You should see this roof, Jakey," Andy said with a manic grin in his voice. "'S really steep. Like crazy steep. But there's a smaller building next to it, yanno? Maybe ten-foot drop? If I had my skateboard, bet I could make it. 'S in my room."

I could hear that calculating tone in his voice, even though he was drunk. Drunk, risk-taking Andy terrified me.

"Listen to me," I said as firmly as I could. "You're not sober. You're not thinking straight right now. You can't judge distances and all that shit when you're drunk. Do *not* attempt a stunt of any kind. Can you please go inside now? Would you do that for me?"

"'M tired, Jake." Andy's voice was so soft I barely heard him over the wind. "I don't want to do this anymore."

Like a movie in my head, I could see him, balancing on the peak of a steep roof on some old New England edifice, toes over the edge. He'd be shit-faced and wobbly. And that wind, God! It sounded hard enough that a gust alone could send him flying. He was so fucking *insane.*

He'd always had this death wish, I realized, something inside him that had its finger on the self-destruct button. He'd reined it in in the past, channeled it into daring feats that were, nevertheless, planned out and not as dangerous as they appeared. Now I heard the pain in his voice, the *loneliness*, and I knew it wouldn't take much for him to take that step into thin air. Oh God, I knew it wouldn't. Andy Tyler, daredevil.

Fuck, fuck, fuck. I curled up a little, pain seizing my gut. My fist clenched around the phone.

Sierra's eyes were begging me, asking what she could do. I muted the call momentarily and whispered to Sierra. "Call Harvard. Tell them they might have a jumper and give his name. He said he's on 'Hastings.' Probably his residence."

With a sharp nod, Sierra left the room.

"Andy?" I had to keep him on the phone. "Hey, listen to me. Can you hear me?"

"Yeah." The wind howled as if angry that he dared try to hold a conversation.

"Okay, just listen. You have options. All right? It doesn't have to be the way you and your dad set it up. People change. Plans change.

It's as easy as . . . as sending an email of resignation to the school. Or changing your major. Or transferring to Stanford so we can be close." *Or coming out*, I thought, but I didn't want to freak him out even more. "Just think about it, Andy. If you don't like what's going on, we'll fix it. Okay? We'll fix it. That's all."

"But . . . what else would I do? If I left school now the only thing I'd be qualified for is a law clerk or maybe a little league coach. I can't survive on fifteen dollars an hour!"

He sounded so anguished. Sometimes I really wanted to kill Mr. Tyler. His obsession with Andy's future had given Andy a black-and-white, all-or-nothing perspective. I made myself stay calm though. What was important right now was getting Andy off that roof.

"Hey," I joked. "Law clerks can be hot. And famous too. Remember that movie with Julia Roberts?"

"This is not funny, Jake!" Andy roared, tears in his voice.

Okay. So humor was not the right way to go. Got it.

"I'm sorry. Just . . . will you stop putting so much pressure on yourself? There are other things in life besides big degrees and money. Even if you did make fifteen dollars an hour, you'd be fine. Hell, come out and live with me in California and surf! Give yourself time to figure out what you want to do. I've got a job. I can take care of us for a while. But if you do something stupid right now, like ride your goddamn skateboard off that roof drunk, or take a header, you'll be dead. Do you hear me? *The end.* And then we'll never have the chance to work it out. Andy, *please.*"

I heard him breathing hard on the other end of the phone. When he spoke, his voice was softer. "Miss you so much. Miss being with you. God, Jake. Feels like someone ripped my guts out." His teeth chattered, like he was shaking apart.

A sob caught in my throat. I swallowed it. Crying would be completely useless right now. I sank down so I was sitting at the base of the sink. "I know. Me too. God, Andy. I swear, I miss you so much it feels like I'm dying sometimes."

"Everything, everything, *everything* is wrong, and it's all so tangled up, and I don't know how to change it or what else I'd do even if I could!"

"That's fine! You don't have to know that right now. Okay? We'll look at one issue at a time. I'll help you. Just . . . please, Andy." My heart pulsed raw and open, right there. I had nothing left with which to hold on to him, so I had no choice. "I love you. God help me, I love you so much. If something happened to you, it would kill me too. So please, don't. Go inside and we'll work it out. You and me. The Andy and Jake Show."

I heard him sniffling. "You'll help me figure it out?"

"I will, yes, absolutely." I nodded adamantly, as if he could see me.

There was a soft noise on the other end of the phone, maybe a sigh, but I couldn't make it out over the wind. I could sense, though, that something had shifted. "Prob'bly is too far," he muttered. I heard the scraping sound of footsteps over tile. He was walking across the roof. *Oh, thank God. Just please don't let him fall.*

"I need you," Andy said quietly. His voice sounded less frenzied, more in control.

"I can be there." I sat up straighter and wiped at my eyes. "Let me book a flight. I should be able to get there by tomorrow."

"No. Hang on."

There was a sound that must have been a stiff window closing. And then the wind was gone. I shuddered with relief. *Oh my God.* I was covered in sweat. Maybe the situation over there hadn't been as dire as it'd sounded. But I could swear I saw headlines like *Student jumps to his death.* And if that student had been Andy Tyler, would anyone really be surprised?

"Andy?" I prompted when he didn't speak.

"Don't book a flight. Maybe . . . maybe I'll come out there. I dunno. Have to figure it out. But meanwhile, we can talk? You don't hate me?"

"No! I don't hate you. Of course we can talk," I assured him. "As much as you want."

"Only not now, because I'm going to be sick." He moaned. I wondered what the hell he'd been drinking.

"Are you near your room?"

Over the phone, I heard the sound of sirens and footsteps on stairs. Andy panted, "Did you . . . call someone?"

I laughed. "Yeah, you crazy bastard. You about scared me to death. I swear to God, Andy, if you hurt yourself before I get my hands on you again, I *will* kill you."

"Glad you still care, Jake," Andy said quietly.

Then there were voices and the magical soundtrack of Andy puking his guts out.

Chapter
TWENTY-ONE

ANDY

When I arrived at Abe & Louie's in downtown Boston, my mom was already seated and waiting for me. I'd called her to ask if we could meet for lunch and talk, and it had been her choice of venue.

Abe & Louie's was an upscale Boston classic with dark-mahogany booths and waiters dressed in tan coats, white shirts, and ties. Their uniforms looked like they hadn't changed since the 1950s. The place cooked a mean steak, but I was too nervous to care about food. I was dreading the conversation, but it had to happen. It might be dramatic to say my life depended on it, but it really did.

I slipped into the booth, and my mom kissed my cheek hello.

"There's my beautiful son. Are you feeling all right?" She looked me over and placed the back of her cool hand on my cheek to check for fever. As if the only reason I'd ask her to lunch were if I were terminally ill.

Then again, maybe that was the reason I'd invited her to lunch.

"I'm fine," I insisted.

My mom's brown eyes looked worried. She was a tiny woman, five foot two and petite all over. Her hair, black with a few silver strands, was kept short, but it was curly and sometimes frizzy, despite lots of product. She was on the plain side, an überintellectual. Her large-framed gold glasses were on the table. I swore, she carried them more than she wore them. She had on a fitted gray business suit with a skirt and jacket and a purple blouse underneath. Her only jewelry consisted of her wedding rings and two small gold balls in her ears. She was not the high-heels-and-diamonds type of woman.

"Is this about Harvard? Your classes? How are you getting along with your professors?" she queried. Her gaze was far too observant. It was intimidating having my mom's full attention, especially given what I had to say.

"Classes are fine." I drummed my fingers on the table nervously. "Well. Not really. That's why I wanted to talk to you. I need your advice."

"Advice about what?"

I forced a smile. "My area of study. Life. Love. The universe and everything." I tried to make it sound lighthearted. Not sure I succeeded.

She rubbed her lip and regarded me with more interest now—and more worry. "I thought you and your dad had your curriculum all figured out. You're no longer sure about it?"

I shook my head. "Very much not sure. In fact, I'm fairly certain I don't want to be where I am." It was harder to say out loud than I'd expected. But I meant every word.

"You're no longer interested in corporate law?"

"I wasn't ever that interested in corporate law," I admitted. "But I thought it would give me a secure future. You know how dad is about all that."

She nodded. "He is. That's not a bad thing, Andy."

"No, it's not," I agreed hurriedly. "And I appreciate everything he's done for me. Only now that I'm in the classes, well . . . right now is the time to pick my schedule for next term. I just wanted to . . ." I took a heavy breath. "Wanted to talk to you. About how can you stand it, doing contracts all day, every day? I know you have your pro bono work, but doesn't it get difficult to stay motivated at your regular job when you're doing something you hate?"

The waiter came just then, naturally, and took our order. I ordered the petite fillet with a side salad instead of fries since my mother was watching. She ordered an entrée salad with salmon.

After the waiter left, my mom leaned toward me over the booth, her hands folded at the edge of the table. "Andy, first of all, where did you get the idea that I hate writing contracts?"

"Well . . . I just assumed. It's pretty boring stuff."

She shook her head. "I went into corporate law because it interests me. Protecting my clients, looking for language or clauses that are potentially harmful, foreseeing contingencies and providing for them . . . it's a puzzle, a challenge. I enjoy my work. If contract law doesn't interest you that way, then no, you shouldn't be planning a career in it."

I looked at her in surprise. The way she talked, she sounded honestly passionate.

"But . . . I always thought your heart was in your pro bono work. I thought your work for A. A. & Young was just for money."

She gave me a funny look. "I am passionate about my pro bono work. And, of course, I wouldn't be with A. A. & Young if I wasn't paid very, very well. Because I'm worth it, and I save my clients millions. That doesn't mean I don't enjoy my job."

"Oh." Well there went one long-term assumption. Now I felt idiotic. What was wrong with me that I didn't enjoy it like that?

"Let me ask you this," she said briskly. "If you didn't get a degree in corporate law, what would you do?"

That was the hundred-thousand-dollar question. "I'm not sure. Harvard is a fantastic school, obviously. I'd like to get a law degree from there. But I'm not sure of the area yet. Maybe criminal justice?" I gave a sigh of frustration. "I know Dad says it's way overcrowded and doesn't pay well, and I get that. It's not like I feel a strong calling. I wanted to get your thoughts about it."

So we talked. My mother didn't really have new information, but she asked a lot of questions, and she didn't seem upset at the idea of my changing degrees. At some point I realized that this was the first time I'd ever discussed my future with just my mother alone. She was a lot more open-minded than my dad. Which I pointed out.

"I'm afraid Dad will freak if I change my area of study though." *Among other things.* I sounded like a whiny teenager, so I added, "That is, I'm prepared to stand up to him. But I feel like I need to be absolutely sure what I want before I can do that. I haven't been able to find that kind of clarity."

My mom pushed around the salad in the bowl, looking thoughtful. "Andy, I'm sorry I haven't been more involved in all this. You and your father have always had a very special relationship, and I knew he was good at working with you when it came to your education. So I let him do it. I should have paid more attention."

I blinked in surprise. "It's fine. I know you have a lot on your plate."

A strange expression crossed her face. Guilt maybe? She pressed her lips together. "What about your personal life? If you're thinking about changing your career path, that's something you should discuss with your future partner as well. Are you seeing anyone? Wasn't there a girl named Amber?"

"We broke up at the beginning of summer."

"Oh. Well, there, see. I should have known that." She looked genuinely regretful.

This was the perfect opening for the other thing I'd wanted to talk to her about. My throat went dry. "Speaking of significant others . . . how would you feel if I told you the person I'm interested in is . . ." I took a deep breath ". . . a guy? Jake, in fact."

For the first time, possibly ever, I'd managed to shock my mother. She stared at me, mouth hanging open. She finally raised an eyebrow, picked up her glass, and took a big swig of sparkling water. "Okay. That's interesting. How long have the two of you been together?"

"It happened over the summer. When we were at the cottage."

"But the feelings have been going on longer than that? On your side? His side?" She was impersonal now, collecting facts. And I didn't mind. I really wanted her professional opinion.

"He told me he's been in love with me for years."

"And you?"

What I felt about Jake was so big and so raw and so all over the place, it was hard to put into coherent sentences. But I tried to be honest. "Jake has always been my best friend. I guess now and then I'd have a brief, uh, thought about being . . . more with him. But it wasn't a serious consideration until recently. I know that being with Jake would change everything. But . . . I don't know if I can live without him."

I thought of Friday night, when my misery had gotten so bad I'd drunk a half a bottle of vodka and nearly taken a header off the roof of Hastings. I felt better now, having talked to Jake over the weekend on the phone. We both agreed that we wanted to be together if and when that became possible. But nothing had been settled, and I had to get my act together quickly.

My mom was looking at me with an unhappy frown.

"Are you angry?" I asked her.

She shook her head. "Andy, I don't care if you're gay—"

"Bisexual."

"Bisexual, then. But in our current political climate, you'll face difficulty, and I am sorry for that." She sighed. "Then again, I suppose being Jewish has its challenges as well."

"But we don't have a choice about being Jewish. Since I'm bisexual, most people will assume I have a choice who I end up with. Dad will."

She gave me an odd look. Then she put down her fork and leaned back in the booth, her face serious. "Have I ever told you the story about how I met your father?"

"No."

"I was twenty-one. There was a party at Vassar, and your dad crashed it. We met and talked for a long time, and by the end of the night he'd asked for my number. Everyone told me that he was bad news, a gold digger, only interested in me because of my family's money."

"Are you serious?" I laughed.

Mom smiled sadly. "Oh yes. You know your dad came from a very poor family, don't you?"

"Yeah." I realized I didn't know very much about his childhood. "How come we never visit his side of the family? Dad always makes excuses."

"He doesn't get along with his parents. We went to see them in West Virginia shortly after we were married."

"Really? What were they like?"

She made a half-bemused, half-sad face. "They were . . . rednecks, I guess. Really very poor. His dad was on disability, some sort of back injury, and his mother didn't work. Your dad paid his own way through college. It wasn't a comfortable visit." She pursed her lips. "They thought he was 'too big for his britches,' as his dad put it. And they were not happy that he'd brought home this plain little Jewish girl."

"Are you serious? They were anti-Semitic?"

"Oh, yes. His dad had a Confederate flag in the yard. It didn't make any sense to try to carry on a relationship with them, so we didn't. It's a shame but . . . Anyway. I was telling you how all my friends and family warned me about your dad. He was the most handsome man I'd ever seen. And, well, I'd had very little male attention up until then."

Her eyes grew fond. "You take after him. Tall, blond, blue-eyed. Lord. He could charm the skin off a snake. He certainly charmed me. Your dad always knew what he wanted."

There was something in her voice, a tension. *Had* my dad been a gold digger? My mom's great-grandfather had started a chain of department stores on the East Coast called Derringer's and had made millions. Her father wasn't in the direct line of succession for the main fortune, but he'd owned a few airlines in his day before they'd been bought out and merged with United. Knowing my dad, it wouldn't surprise me if all of that had figured into his decision to court my mom. He was so practical. And that made me feel kind of awful for her.

"He loved you though, right?" I asked.

She gave me a surprised look. "Of course! Well. Not the same way I loved him, I suppose. But we built a life together. We had you. I have no regrets."

"That's good."

But was it? It would suck to be crazy about someone and then figure out they viewed you more as an investment. Come to think of it, I'd never seen my parents be overtly affectionate. Was that why my mom worked so many hours?

"So! Advice about Jake. I could sit here and treat you like a client, Andy."

"Maybe you should."

"No, I don't think so." She gave me a sad little smile. "I can tell you what I've learned from having years' worth of clients. When there's a conflict between what's practical and what the heart wants, the heart usually wins. And when it doesn't, there's regret. A lot of regret." She shook her head. "I guess what I'm trying to say is: you can make yourself a list of rules to follow. But if your heart isn't in it, you won't be happy. It's as simple as that."

She was right. I'd faced some harsh schooling to that effect lately.

"As a lawyer, what I'd recommend is that you do your homework. What would life with Jake look like? Where would you live? How would it affect your schooling, your job, your social circle, your bank account? Think of it as a business plan. What's the best-case scenario? The worst-case? Follow your heart, but at least put your head through its paces."

"Okay," I said slowly. "That's good advice."

She bit her lip and frowned. I had a feeling I wasn't going to like what she was about to say.

"What is it?" I asked.

"I want to ask you something, and I'd appreciate it if you'd hear me out."

I nodded, my apprehension rising.

"These . . . stunts you've engaged in from time to time. Like the firecracker trick that nearly disabled you for life."

"Mom—"

"No, listen. I know Jake has usually been involved in those stunts. Is he the instigator?"

"No. It's usually me." I felt a need to defend Jake. And, anyway, it was true.

"Are you sure? What about that time you jumped a cliff at the quarry on your motorbike?"

I stared at her. "You knew about that?"

She gave me her *don't be foolish* look. "Andrew, it's on your YouTube channel."

"You watch my YouTube channel?" I was horrified. What the fuck? Parental intrusion. Was that even legal?

"Do you want to discuss that right now, or do you want to focus on what's actually relevant today?"

"Fine. So you saw the quarry video."

"I saw the quarry video. And thank God I had no idea you were doing it at the time or I would have had a heart attack."

"Well the quarry was definitely my idea."

She nodded thoughtfully. "Was there a reason? Were you acting out or . . . rebelling against your father and me? Was it about your schooling? I'm just trying to understand. Because I know these stunts involve Jake, and I'm wondering if there's some message there that should be part of your thought process on this."

I was about to deny it. Of course it wasn't Jake's fault! But then I thought better of it. I thought back to the quarry jump. Senior year. I remembered that panicky, itchy feeling, that need to do something, something daring and crazy. I'd been upset about something . . .

College. That was when we'd been getting acceptance letters to the schools we'd applied to. Jake had decided to go to NYU, and I'd been accepted there but also to MIT and Yale. At the time, Dad wanted me to pick one of those.

I stared at my mom in astonishment. "The quarry. I was freaking out because I had to lock down a college, and I wanted to go to NYU with Jake but Dad wasn't happy about it."

My brain scrambled for other dares. The subway-surfing one. That still made me cringe. Jake had been so pissed off. That had been our junior year of college, and I'd been . . .

Trying to get Jake's attention. That's when he was seeing Kevin. Shit.
The skateboard parkour our junior year of high school.
Jake's first real girlfriend, Denise. God, I hated her.

Even the stupid caterpillar stunt had been about Jake. It was the end of ninth grade and I was upset because he was supposed to go to Nevada to visit his dad over the summer, and I wouldn't be able to see him for months. I remembered worrying that he'd decide to transfer there, or his parents would force him to, and I'd never see him again.

Something must have shown on my face. My mother put down her fork and leaned forward, studying my eyes. "Looks like you just had an epiphany."

My chest felt hot. "Jake. It's always been about Jake."

"Well that doesn't sound very healthy."

"No! I mean, it's my fault. But I push. I push when I . . . when I feel like I'm losing him. Because I . . ." The truth of it hit me between the eyes.

She leaned back and took a sip of coffee, her face smoothing out. Her eyes were compassionate and resigned. "I guess you have your answer."

I nodded. I had my answer. At last. At last I was sure.

Chapter
TWENTY-TWO

JAKE

The weekend of Sierra's wedding arrived and forced my head out of my own drama. Since that insane phone call with Andy, when he'd been drunk and on a roof, he and I had talked almost every day. But we'd talked mostly about my job and his degree and hadn't settled anything between us. He'd told me he was "trying to work things out."

Still. There were lots of *I miss you*s, and assurances that we both wanted to see each other, badly. Our relationship had shifted, if only on the phone. It was romantic. It was sexual. Andy wasn't even pretending we were just friends. And, for now, that eased my pain and heartbreak considerably, even if I still had no clue how, or if, it would work out.

With Sierra's wedding imminent, and Andy trying to figure out his schooling before it became too late to change his course load, neither of us seemed likely to get away for a trip across the country anytime soon.

Sierra and Tom's rehearsal happened and then the rehearsal dinner. Mom was in town, staying at a motel since we had no spare room at the apartment. My dad was there, sans his second wife and two kids, and several of my aunts and uncles, along with a bunch of Sierra's friends from high school and college. It was a madhouse.

I didn't hear from Andy the day of the wedding, which was scheduled for five o'clock. And then, when I was walking back down the aisle after the ceremony with Linda, one of Sierra's bridesmaids, on my arm, I saw him at the back of the church. He was dressed in a rose tie, white shirt, and navy-blue suit that brought out the blue of his eyes. He looked so stunning, he stole my breath away.

I stared at him as I walked by, and as soon as I could, I found him in the crowd outside the church. He didn't even say hello, just pulled me into a hug. The feel of him against me made my bruised and battered heart gallop in my chest.

He whispered in my ear, "Damn, you clean up nice. I wanted to run up there and steal you away in the middle of the 'I dos'"

I laughed, picturing it, and feeling so damned happy that he was here. "You should have. Would have made the day memorable, like those fainting groom videos."

I pulled away to look at him, hardly believing he was really here. "When did you arrive? Why didn't you tell me you were coming?"

"I wanted to surprise you."

Andy's expression was odd—he was glowing with a kind of peace I'd never seen in him before, but there was a nervous look in his eyes too. Did he think I might turn him away?

"I'm glad you're here," I said earnestly. "God, there's so much I want to show you! How long are you—"

"Jake? We're taking pictures!" My mom came up to us. "Hello, Andy! I didn't know you were coming for the wedding." My mom was in a good mood, and she sounded welcoming. She had no idea what all had gone on between Andy and me. Some things it was just best not to tell your mother.

"Hi, Mrs. Masterson. I thought I'd surprise Jake."

"Well that's nice." She placed a hand on my arm. "Come on, hon. Everyone's waiting."

"You're not going anywhere, right?" I asked Andy.

"How about I'll see you at the reception?" He smiled sheepishly.

"Oh. Okay. You know where it is?"

"Yup. Sierra texted me the address, and I have GPS in the rental car."

"Cool. The Planinator strikes again."

Andy winked at me—winked! Like he was actually flirting. Embarrassingly, my stomach fluttered on cue. "See you there."

I let my mom drag me away, but I was confused. He'd been texting with Sierra about coming and she hadn't told me? I didn't get a chance to ask her since the entire wedding party was soon being posed like Barbie dolls over and over and over again.

The reception was at a rambling Italian restaurant with Spanish decor, a fountain out front, an open bar, band stage, and several large rooms you could wander between. I'd scouted it out earlier with Bridezilla, I mean, Sierra. The best part of the place was the setting. It was next to a vineyard, and there were mounded California hills in the distance, golden brown against the green of the extensive fields of vines. It was well after six when we all arrived in a limousine, and the light had a soft, shimmering quality that was magical. I admired the view for a moment before pushing my way inside to find Andy.

I found him standing by the bar. I grabbed his hand and led him outside onto a back patio that overlooked the vineyard. It was thankfully quiet out there.

"I can't believe you came!" I told him, breathless and excited.

"I didn't want to wait any longer to see you." His eyes were warm as he cupped my face in both hands and slowly kissed me. The kiss was sweet, his tongue and lips sucking at me softly, but it made waves of want roll through me. It was so familiar, and at the same time, precious. I never thought I'd feel his kiss again.

It struck me that he was kissing me in public. True, no one else was on the patio, but people could see us through the glass restaurant doors. Plus he'd made the romantic gesture of flying all the way to California for Sierra's wedding. I felt an injection of hope so intense it frightened me.

Don't go too fast, Jake. This could still blow up.

I pulled away and studied his face.

"Why do you look so worried?" he asked with a bemused look.

"I don't know how serious you are about this. And I'm . . . Just don't fuck me around, Andy. Please." My stomach ached with doubt, with the painful gap between want and fear.

He frowned. "I know I hurt you, Jake. I'm really sorry about that."

I shook my head. "I know. You already apologized on the phone. It's just . . ."

"Do you think I'd come all this way if I wasn't serious?"

I huffed a laugh. "That's a dumb question. I think you would do just about anything."

He grinned. "You have a point. How can I prove it to you?" There was a twinkle in his voice, like he had his own ideas. But I was more than happy to offer suggestions.

"Okay . . . Let's see. I dare you to slow dance with me tonight. In there, in front of all the wedding guests, for an entire song."

Andy's eyes took on that dangerously reckless light. "That's all? You're daring me to give you one dance?"

"Yes, but it has to be to ABBA," I deadpanned.

He looked pained.

"I'm kidding! Any slow dance. And you have to hold me closer to your body than two feet."

The dare wasn't only on Andy. I still wasn't out to my mom, dad, assorted aunts and uncles, or my coworkers at Neverware, some of whom were at the wedding. But it had always been my intention to be, so this seemed like a great way to kill all those birds with one stone. The question was: was Andy prepared to own it?

He smirked. "Dare accepted. Let's go."

He took my hand and turned back to the patio doors.

"I meant later! No one's dancing yet!" I protested, laughing as he tugged me into the restaurant.

The reception was still in the early wander-around-and-gab stage. Sierra and Tom were chatting with people by the doors. The waitstaff were moving around with hors d'oeuvres. But Andy didn't seem to care. He dragged me to the middle of the empty dance floor, left me there, and went up to the band. Tom had hired a four-piece group of guys with drums, electric guitars, and a keyboard who, according to Sierra, could play anything. They were playing some low instrumental soft rock at the moment. Andy spoke to one of them.

I looked around self-consciously. What was he doing? The dork. He wanted to dance *now*?

I caught Sierra's eye across the room. She smiled at me and gave me a nod. *Go ahead.* Her face looked anxious.

Okay, this was weird. My pulse began to race.

The band started playing something slow. Andy came up to me and took me into his arms. It was strange, with his hand on top and him leading. I'd never danced with another guy before. But that worry amounted to a momentary burst of awkward nerves, and then I just let go and let him lead. God knew, he always *had* led when it came to our craziest moments.

"Andy . . ." I looked around. Everyone was watching us.

"It's okay, Jake," he said in my ear. But he sounded nervous too.

And then I heard the lyrics the band was singing. It was Ed Sheeran. Andy had picked *this* song? Surprised, I pulled back far enough to look at his face. "'Thinking Out Loud'?"

He shrugged a little, as if saying he couldn't help it. "Just listen."

He tugged me in again with his arm on my back, and I let him. It felt too good to be close to him. And, anyway, no one had ever done anything this romantic for me in my life.

I closed my eyes and tried to calm down. All the systems in my body were in a state of five-alarm fire, overwhelmed with scatter-shot emotions: disbelief, nerves, longing, embarrassment at being stared at, love . . . There was definitely love. A hot mass of it sitting on my chest.

This felt bigger than just a dance. Bigger than coming out even. I worried about Andy making such a statement. I didn't want him to regret it or pull away.

But I decided to cling to the love and dismiss the rest. Andy was doing this for me, declaring himself in front of the world, and I wanted to appreciate every minute of it. I sank close to his body as we moved, resting my chest against him, the top of my head leaning against the side of his jaw. I felt him nuzzle my hair.

God, I'd missed him so much. I'd gotten used to the feeling of his body against me during our time at the cottage. It'd been torture when he'd been ripped away, like losing part of myself. Now he was here, and there was so much *intent* in the way he held me. No longer in a casual or heated way. Not *my best mate, Jake*. There was something new in his hands. Like I was important.

His body was warm against me, his hands slightly damp.

The song lyrics ripped out my guts as Ed sang about finding true love in the same place you'd been all along. Did Andy mean that?

Was he talking about him and me? Or maybe it was the only slow song he could think of. I didn't want to assume too much.

He spoke into my ear. "I was talking to my mom about us the other day."

"You were? You did?" I was surprised.

I felt him nod. "Yes. And while I was telling her about us, I realized I've always loved you, Jake. Even back when we were eating caterpillars, I was crazy about you."

"You did? You were?"

My knees went a little weak. I opened my eyes so I didn't fall over. Everyone was still watching us, though I was only vaguely aware of them. The song was winding down. I gripped his hand harder, not wanting to let him go.

"I was. And I want you to know that I have permission from Sierra to do this next part at her reception."

"What next part?" I asked faintly, just as the music ended.

Andy released me and sank to one knee. I covered my mouth with a hand to keep in the scream.

He help up a small black box. Inside was a thick and heavy platinum ring.

I thought I might throw up. I'd never been so shocked in my life.

The band went into some low instrumental thing, and it was suddenly quiet enough that I could hear my pounding heart.

Andy tried to smile up at me, but it wobbled. His eyes were burning blue. "It turns out I'm miserable without you. So miserable, I was hoping you'd promise me we'd never have to be apart again. I love you. Whatever it takes for us to build a life together, I'll do it."

"Oh my God!" I said, brilliantly.

"We don't have to get married soon if you're not ready. I just want you to know that, ultimately, I'm committed to you. You're my white picket fence, Jake Masterson, and you always will be."

Somewhere people were clapping. Somewhere, my mother asked "When did *this* happen?" in a loud voice. Somewhere there was sunshine, and birds, and a whole planet full of people doing stuff. But it honestly felt like no one else existed at that moment but Andy and me.

I sank down into a squat in front of him and closed my hand over his wrist. "I'll never stop loving you," I told him, my voice suspiciously wet. "So 'forever' sounds pretty good to me. And you're absolutely insane, by the way."

He smiled, bright and beautiful. "Well, I wouldn't want to bore you."

I took the box, threw my arms around him, and kissed him.

Chapter TWENTY-THREE

ANDY

Sierra's wedding reception went by in a blur. There were lots of congratulations, worried scolding from Jake's mom, who was nonetheless tentatively happy for us, a reluctant handshake from his dad, food, cake, and a considerable amount of wine.

I danced with Sierra. She looked like Jake, with dark hair and eyes, and she was smart as aces too.

"Don't let him down again," she warned me sternly. "He was a mess when he got to California."

I was glad to hear that. I certainly had been a mess, and it was nice to think Jake had missed me just as much. "We're no good apart," I said simply.

I was riding a high. *Jake said yes!* We agreed that we needed to be together, always. And that was everything. As long as I didn't lose Jake, nothing else was all that important. I spun Sierra once around. She was so light.

She laughed, but she wasn't put off her sisterly duty. "Will you move to California or what?"

"Good question. I don't know yet."

Her face softened then, as if by admitting I didn't have the answers, I deserved her sympathy. "It's all right. You're both smart guys. You'll work it out. And you've got your families' support." An expression of doubt crossed her face. "Don't you? Are your parents okay with you and Jake?"

That fast, my glow threatened to be ruined. Things were far from settled in Boston. But I didn't want to think about that, not tonight. Tonight all I wanted to think about was Jake.

"Hey, this is your wedding. You should be thinking about your future with Tom."

A huge smile took over her face. "You're right. I'm the important one today. How could I forget?"

Fortunately, she stopped asking me questions after that.

When my dance with Sierra was over, I found Jake and pulled him onto the dance floor. The band was playing "Twist and Shout" and we went a little nuts. Jake always had been a good dancer. He was better than me, the bum. But now I could appreciate his moves in a whole new way.

That's my boyfriend, I kept thinking, watching him. *That's my fiancé.*

The idea was both bizarre and wonderful, like a short story I'd read years ago where the sun only came out once every fifty years, and seeing it was both frightening and the most precious thing ever. I felt free. So many worries about my future dissolved knowing Jake was a part of it. He was my best friend. I'd always love him, always trust him, and he'd always have my back no matter what life threw at us. But there were still some heavy unknowns.

We danced until most everyone had left and the band packed up. Then we went back to Sierra's apartment. Thankfully, we had it to ourselves because she and Tom were staying in a fancy hotel for their wedding night.

When it was just the two of us alone and Jake started kissing me, it felt like we'd never left the cottage—the feeling of his hands on my skin, the way his tongue sucked lightly at my mouth and then began to thrust as he got more and more desperate. But there was something new about the sex too, a depth and seriousness that almost hurt. It felt too overwhelmingly important. Like I wasn't sure if I wanted to moan in ecstasy or run away from the force of the emotion, maybe hide in the bathroom and get myself under control before I did something stupid like cry. But then Jake cracked a joke and went down on me, all devious looking and sexy, and I forgot to feel awkward. When he straddled my lap and lowered himself onto my dick, it was with a little growl of lust and a focused look that I knew as well as I knew my own skin.

And I knew then that I never wanted to be anywhere except with Jake Masterson.

Holding him close to me that night, I knew that whatever happened, being with Jake was worth it. But hopefully the future could still be bright. The Planinator had a secret weapon, after all.

I just hoped I could get that weapon to work for me and not shoot my foot off.

We flew back to the East Coast on a red-eye Monday morning and went straight to my dad's office from the airport. I'd talked Jake into taking a couple of days off work and coming back to Boston with me. It was our future now, and he needed to be in on the plans. Besides, I didn't want to argue with my dad about my relationship with Jake. I wanted to present it as a done deal.

My father had worked for Paine Webber once upon a time, but he'd left with two other hotshots to create their own financial planning firm. MRT Futures was in a converted old mansion not far from downtown Boston. Everything about the place screamed "old money," from the impeccably painted turrets to the shiny brass plate by the front door.

MRT Futures
Graham Alsen, AIFA, APMA, APP
Bryan Tyler, AEP, AFA, AIFA
Richard Trunbill, AIFA, AAMA

"They've really got the alphabet covered," Jake joked as we walked up on the porch. "But I was kinda hoping for a GFG."

"GFG?"

"Gay Futures Guaranteed."

I laughed. "You're such a dweeb. No wonder I love you."

"Yeah, that's nice," Jake said dismissively. "But what I really want is permission to stay out here on the porch while you talk to the old man."

"Nope," I said, opening the door.

The firm's receptionist, Judith, smiled at me when we walked into the office.

"Good to see you, Andy. Your dad's waiting for you, and he doesn't have a client meeting until ten o'clock. Would you like some coffee, either of you?"

Jake looked about as tense as I felt, and it couldn't be blamed on the lack of sleep on the plane. I interlaced his fingers with mine. "That would be great. Black for me, and Jake takes cream. By the way, this is Jake Masterson, my fiancé. Jake, this is Judith."

"Hi, Judith." Jake offered his right hand, which fortunately wasn't the one I was holding.

Judith didn't even blink, though I knew I'd surprised her. She shook Jake's hand. "Nice to meet you, Jake. I'll go get that coffee. You can go on in, Andy."

Jake tried to pull his hand away as we walked down the hall, but I kept it locked in mine. He gave me a fierce look. I gave him a fierce look back. I opened the door to my dad's office and we walked in.

As one of the partners of the firm, his office was cushy. It had once been a parlor with a big bay window. His cherry antique desk was enormous and very clean with a single organizer of folders, a bunch of expensive black pens in a leather holder, a leather notebook, and a sleek computer monitor.

He stood up when Jake and I walked in. His eyes dropped to our hands, and his jaw tightened. There was such profound disappointment on his face that I felt immediately sorry. Damn. The urge to please him was practically primal. I resisted it.

"Your mother warned me," he said flatly. "I take it that wasn't just *convenient sex* I walked in on at the cottage after all?"

His tone of voice got under my skin. He made it sound like I'd been purposefully lying or, worse, didn't know my own mind. I pushed down my anger.

"No. Jake and I worked things out, and now we're together." I glanced at Jake and saw him swallow nervously. "We'd like to talk to you about our plans if you think we can do that productively."

I used my softest, most reasonable tone. Jake and I stood near the door to make it clear I was prepared to walk out if need be. Jake's hand was clutched like a reluctantly captured fish in mine, but I gave it a squeeze. *It's all right. Be strong.*

"Jake came all this way, and I cleared my schedule, so there's no point delaying it. Sit down." My dad waved at the chairs in front of his desk with an irritated gesture.

That was probably as good an invitation as I was likely to get, so I walked to the chairs with Jake and finally let go of his hand. The dark wood and leather were not spaced conveniently to keep hold of him and, besides, I'd made my point.

"Thanks for seeing us, Mr. Tyler," Jake said as he sat down. His voice sounded steady, but I knew he was dreading this. So was I.

My dad glanced at him and nodded. Hell, my dad was probably dreading it too.

He turned to me. "What's going on with Harvard? Have you dropped out of your classes too?"

I replied calmly. "No, I took Friday off to go see Jake, but I haven't dropped classes. Everything is fine there, but that's part of what I want to discuss with you. First, though . . ." I turned my head to look at Jake. He looked back at me, his eyes going wide in an *oh shit, this is it* comical look that lightened my spirits enough to get the words out. "I asked Jake to marry me, and he said yes. We're not sure when yet, but we don't want to wait too long due to the political climate. We want to make it legal while we can."

That went over like a lead balloon. When I looked back at my dad, his face had gone white. His voice sounded strangled. "Perhaps Jake could wait in reception for a few minutes. I'd like to discuss this with you alone, Andrew."

Jake started to stand up, but I reached out and put a hand on his arm. "No. We're all adults here. Go ahead and say what you want to say."

Jake sat down. He gave me a dirty look that said he would have been thrilled to escape. I gave him a dirty look back.

"Very well." My dad appeared to consider his words. "Your mother said you told her you're bisexual."

"That's right."

He leaned forward and went into a reasonable tone of voice. "If that's true, then you have a choice. You could just as easily be happily married to a woman. You do understand that if you're openly gay, that's a brush that will paint everything about you? It will narrow down every job opportunity, eliminate you from a dozen top firms, inform and constrict your social networking. The old boy's network is still incredibly conservative."

"Openly bi, Dad. And I'll find the one firm that doesn't have a problem with it. I only need one. As for a social network, I'll build a progressive one. Look how many celebrities and corporations supported gay marriage. They need lawyers too."

It took everything I had to stay logical. I knew emotion wouldn't impress my dad.

"You can work for progressives without being gay—or bi, but the reverse isn't true. Yes, you only need *one* plum job, but to get that one, you need to have as many options as possible. No offense to Jake, but I don't understand why you—*either* of you—would want to hamstring yourselves like this. You should at least wait a year or two before you take an irreversible step like marriage."

"Okay, listen." I rubbed my face with my hands. I *hated* this, facing my dad head on like this. But it was something I had to get through. "Yes, the administration is more conservative now, but there's also a huge backlash against that. The point is, no one is guaranteed anything. I might just as easily *get* a plum job two years from now because I'm bi and the firm has a directive to be more inclusive, as I could lose it for the same reason. We can't predict everything—"

"Of course not. But—"

"And you married mom in the eighties even though she was Jewish. Anti-Semitism still exists and could easily become worse in the future as well. That didn't stop you."

My dad hesitated, his mouth open in surprise. He closed it. "That's true. But your mother's education, her family background . . . She brought a lot to the table."

The implication pissed me off, but I didn't show it. I reached over and put my hand on Jake's arm. "Jake brings a lot to the table. He's bright, hard-working, graduated at the top of his class in engineering, and has a good career ahead of him. More importantly, I want to be with him forever. He's the one I've chosen, Dad. And that's just the way it is."

I stared at my dad, silently willing him to hear me. Jake put his hand on mine and squeezed a *thank-you*. Or maybe it was a *Wow, you are so getting laid later*. Or even *Great! Can I go now please?*

My dad tapped the desk with his pen for a long moment, staring out the window with a frown, his mouth pursed. I wondered what all my mother had said to him. She seemed to have accepted Jake and me by the time I'd left that lunch with her. I hoped she had my back.

"If you're determined to pursue this path," my dad said at last, "a Harvard degree is more important than ever. Please tell me you see that, both of you."

This time he included both Jake and me in his glare, which made a shot of happiness burble up inside me. Jake's neck was now on my dad's chopping block too? That made me so damn glad!

"I agree." Jake nodded. "Andy should finish his degree at Harvard. It's a huge opportunity."

"Right. So let's talk about that," I said. "Let's push plan A and B and C off the table and talk about plan D. All right?"

"Plan G," Jake put in with a completely straight face.

I bit my lip. "Plan G. Let's discuss plan G."

If my dad caught the reference, he didn't show it. His gaze was different this time, assessing. "I'm listening."

"Right," I said. "So here's our first objective: I want to change my area of focus to sports law."

"Sports law?" My dad looked confused. He shook his head adamantly.

"Just hear me out. It was Jake's idea, actually, and I discussed it with my Harvard adviser last week. It's an up-and-coming field. You can rep athletes with injuries, ball clubs, negotiate sports contracts, advise sports facilities—things like that. It would be a way for me to continue to be involved with sports and still practice law. I'd get my JD from Harvard, but I'd study contract law with a specialization in sports. They've got a whole section of courses on it now."

I saw a hint of hurt in my dad's eyes. That was the first time I'd ever seen that, and it made my chest tighten with guilt.

"Andrew, we spent *years* crafting your goals and your career path. I'm deeply concerned about just throwing that all out the window just because you're—" he glanced at Jake "—emotionally raw at the moment."

I was going to speak, but Jake got there first. "I don't want to intrude, sir, but I've known Andy for a long time. And, for just as long, he hasn't felt any conviction about corporate law. He's discussed it with me a hundred times over the past four years." He gave me an encouraging smile. "You know he loves sports, and this would allow him to still be around all that. I've never seen him this excited about law before. And I'm sure you agree with me that he's more likely to be successful in a field he's passionate about."

"Hmm." My dad made a noncommittal noise, but he appeared to be listening.

"Plus, it's not really that big a change," Jake continued. "It's still a JD from Harvard, after all. If he ever changed his mind, he could do straight corporate law with that degree. He still has to take all the core classes."

I pushed a little more. "I know you and I spent a lot of years on my plan, and I really appreciate all your help, but it can't be set in stone. I didn't know at sixteen or eighteen what I know about myself right now, or that sports law was even an option. This is the time, right now, when I'm just starting Harvard, for me to realign the plan. Because if I'm not happy writing business contracts ten hours a day, then what is the point?"

"The *point* is security. The point is this." He waved his hand as if to indicate his office. "The point is having a net for retirement. Or for serious illness, or—"

"Dad." I held up my hand to stop him. "I know you want to protect me and advise me, because that's what you do. But Jake and I both have excellent educations. There will always be work for Jake in technology, and I *will* be able to get work with my JD. It may not be a partnership with one of the top ten firms in Manhattan or Boston, but that's fine. I don't need a fancy lifestyle."

"And we have you to help us with a retirement plan, Mr. Tyler," Jake said, his brown eyes hopeful. "I know you're the best."

Bless his conniving little heart. That was my wingman.

My dad sat back, closed his eyes, and rubbed them with his fingers. But I could sense a resignation about him. Which was good—I hoped. Please, God, let it be good.

With a world-weary sigh he sat up, opened up his leather-bound notebook, and grabbed a pen. He wrote *#1 Sports Law* on his pad. I nearly crowed. It felt like a victory.

"So Andrew will remain at Harvard." He looked between Jake and me with professional interest. "What about you, Jake. Will you continue to work in California?"

"Preferably not." Jake leaned forward a little. "I'd like to find a comparable engineering job near here."

"How much are you making?"

"My salary is $65K."

My dad wrote down *#2 Relocation*, and under it with a bullet point, *Jake $65K*. "There's a growing technology sector in Boston," he said briskly. "Did you apply to anything local when you were looking for work?"

And my dad was off. Jake talked to him easily, and his hand settled comfortably in mine.

As I watched them, I got a lump in my throat and had to blink my eyes. The two parts of my life had come together, and nobody was bloody and nothing had exploded.

Hurrah for the Andy and Jake Show. We'd safely made the jump and were back on solid ground.

Epilogue

Two years later
Jake

The May day was gorgeous and sunny, a particularly fine afternoon for Boston. Yesterday, Andy had graduated from Harvard law school and we'd all gone to his commencement—Andy's parents, my mom, me, and some of our friends. Today his folks were throwing a party for him at their place, a fancy affair with lots of friends of the Tylers and people from his and her work. They were what his dad would call "good contacts." The Tylers' Belmont residence was a huge old brick colonial that had been renovated years ago and had gates, a large lawn, and a garden out back complete with a pool and guesthouse.

It was nothing like the one-bedroom apartment Andy and I shared near the Harvard campus, but I preferred our place by far. It was in a hip little neighborhood with great restaurants, and we could walk everywhere. Plus it was super gay-friendly. I couldn't imagine wanting to live anywhere else.

"You got registered for your fall classes all right?" Andy's dad asked me.

We were standing by the pool, him sipping something like a martini from a short square glass and me just enjoying the sunshine.

"Yup. Though I'm only taking one, that Advanced AI class. Now that Andy's graduated, I thought we could both use a semester that's not so busy."

I'd been taking two classes a semester at MIT toward my master's, on top of working full-time at Strictly Robotics, a company founded by a bunch of MIT graduates. It was all good, but I could use a little more time with my husband.

Andy's dad nodded. "That makes sense. You boys have been working hard."

"Right. Plus Andy will be traveling around New England a lot with his new job. We thought it would be fun if I could go with him once in a while for the weekend."

Andy's mom came up to us, a cocktail in her hand. "Did I hear you say 'travel'? Where are you going, Jake? Oh, can I get you a drink?"

"No, thanks. I just finished a glass of wine. I was telling Bryan that I hope to be able to go with Andy on some of his trips for work. His firm has been repping a number of pro hockey teams, and they told Andy they might send him up to Ontario for their talks with the Canadian Hockey League."

"Oh. I'm sure that would be fun," Andy's mom said unconvincingly.

I laughed. "Yeah, I know Ontario isn't exactly Greece, but we're young and stupid so we like to go just about anywhere. You guys will put us to shame when you come home all tan and . . . and Grecian next month."

Andy's mom looked up at his dad, who was way taller than she was, and gave him a soft smile. He put one arm around her and hugged her.

"I don't know about that," he said. "We may not make it to the beach all that much." He smirked down at her.

Yeah. Okay. *Way* too much information. I really didn't want to think about them *not sunbathing*. Though it did seem like they'd gotten closer lately, and that was nice. Maybe there was something to be said for being empty nesters.

"Andy is suddenly really into ice hockey," I said to change the subject. "He's so excited about working with hockey teams. He dragged me to the skating rink last weekend, and that's about all he'll watch on TV. Go Bruins!"

Andy's mom and dad were still looking at each other and paid me no mind, so I took the opportunity to sneak away. I did need another drink, come to think of it. Or food would be good. There was a buffet set up inside. And where was Andy? Seeing his parents being smoopy made me crave a hug from my man. *Husband*. We were coming up on our year anniversary. Maybe we could celebrate it in Ontario?

I went over to the outside bar to see if he was there, but he wasn't. I did find my mom and her boyfriend, Sherman. He was an older man, not particularly handsome but very sweet. As I accepted their repeated congratulations for Andy's sake, I looked around, wondering where he'd gone.

I finally got away from them and walked around the pool toward the house.

His mom stopped me at the far side of the pool. "Have you seen Andy?" she asked. "There's someone here I want him to meet."

"I don't know," I began. "He was—"

"Jake Masterson!" Andy's voice rang out, loud.

It took me a moment to spot him. He was on the roof of the guesthouse wearing his swim trunks and a T-shirt. Oh boy.

"What're you doing up there, hon?" I called out, shading my eyes to look up at him.

"Andy, come down from there!" said his mother.

Andy threw his arms wide and shook his head. "Nope! Tell me you love me, Jake, or I'll . . . I'll . . . I'll jump into the pool."

"Don't you dare!" called his mother, aghast. "You'll break a leg!"

"Andy, no!" said my mom.

His dad came barging out of the house with plates in both hands. "Andrew, get down from there!"

Everyone at the party stopped their conversations to look up at the guest of honor. There were worried murmurs.

I studied him thoughtfully. Although I shouldn't have been able to detect the wicked sparkle in his eyes from this distance, especially back lit as he was, I so did. Or maybe I just knew it was there. With his arms wide like he was on stage, his body was filled with a happy, excited tension usually reserved for when he came into the bedroom after school hoping for a quickie.

I considered the situation.

He'd freak out our parents, and all the guests, *important* guests. But he'd been such a very good boy. He'd worked so hard through law school, and he hadn't pulled a single stunt since that firecracker dare over two years ago. Besides, he and I had jumped off that guesthouse roof into the pool about a hundred times in our youth when no one was home. It was hardly dangerous. And it *was* his graduation party.

Decision made, I put my palms up in alarm. "Andy, don't! It's too far. You won't make it! Come on down, honey, please?"

"Tell me you love me!" he insisted, backing up and crouching down for a sprint.

"I love you, crazy person! Now don't do it! You'll start your career in a full-leg cast! You'll break your neck hitting the water too hard! You'll drown! You'll—"

Andy ran full tilt toward the edge of the roof, leaped into thin air, rolled into a ball, and landed in the pool with a huge splash.

Everyone on the sides of the pool got wet, including me and his mother.

Andy bobbed to the surface and wiped his face, grinning.

"I need a drink," his mother muttered, walking away.

He swam toward me, and I met him at the edge of the pool. I squatted down and his wet hand grasped my shirt. His eyes were shining.

"I love you too, wingman," he said, and he kissed me.

Dear Reader,

Thank you for reading Eli Easton's *Five Dares*!

We know your time is precious and you have many, many entertainment options, so it means a lot that you've chosen to spend your time reading. We really hope you enjoyed it.

We'd be honored if you'd consider posting a review—good or bad—on sites like **Amazon, Barnes & Noble, Kobo, Goodreads, Twitter, Facebook, Tumblr,** and your blog or website. We'd also be honored if you told your friends and family about this book. Word of mouth is a book's lifeblood!

For more information on upcoming releases, author interviews, blog tours, contests, giveaways, and more, please sign up for our weekly, spam-free newsletter and visit us around the web:

Newsletter: tinyurl.com/RiptideSignup
Twitter: twitter.com/RiptideBooks
Facebook: facebook.com/RiptidePublishing
Goodreads: tinyurl.com/RiptideOnGoodreads
Tumblr: riptidepublishing.tumblr.com

Thank you so much for Reading the Rainbow!

RiptidePublishing.com

Acknowledgments

A tip of the hat to my beta readers Dani, Quinn, Jay, and RJ. I greatly appreciate your ideas and encouragement. Thanks to Amelia for grabbing me by the nape and making me try something new (and for believing in me). And to my Skype bud Jamie, who lets me bounce ideas off him all the way through the process. Thank you for making my writing life so much more enjoyable.

ALSO BY *Eli Easton*

Men of Lancaster County
A Second Harvest
Tender Mercies

Howl at the Moon
How to Howl at the Moon
How to Walk like a Man
How to Wish Upon a Star
How to Save a Life

Sex in Seattle
The Trouble With Tony
The Enlightenment of Daniel
The Mating of Michael

Dreamspun Desires
The Stolen Suitor
Snowblind

Christmas Novellas
Blame it on the Mistletoe
A Prairie Dog's Love Song
Unwrapping Hank
Midwinter Night's Dream
Merry Christmas, Mr. Miggles

Stand Alone Titles
Superhero
Puzzle Me This
Heaven Can't Wait
The Lion and the Crow
Falling Down
Before I Wake

For a full booklist, visit: www.elieaston.com

ABOUT THE Author

Having been, at various times and under different names, a minister's daughter, a computer programmer, a game designer, the author of paranormal thrillers, a fan-fiction writer, an organic farmer, and a profound sleeper, Eli is happy these days writing love stories.

As an avid reader of such, she is tinkled pink when an author manages to combine literary merit, vast stores of humor, melting hotness, and eye-dabbing sweetness into one story. She promises to strive to achieve most of that most of the time. She currently lives on a farm in Lancaster County, Pennsylvania, with her husband, three bulldogs, two cows, a cat, and a potbellied pig. She enjoys reading in all genres and, when she can be pried away from her ipad, hiking and biking.

Eli Easton has published 24 books in m/m romance since 2013. She won the Rainbow Award for Best Contemporary Romance in 2014 (*The Mating of Michael*) and in 2016 (*A Second Harvest*). Her Howl at the Moon series of humorous dog shifter romances have become fan favorites and placed in the Rainbow Awards and the Goodreads M/M Group Reader's Choice awards. She is best known for romances with humor and a lot of heart.

Her website is elieaston.com

Facebook: facebook.com/profile.php?id=100008994061782

Twitter: twitter.com/EliEaston

Goodreads: goodreads.com/author/show/7020231.Eli_Easton

Enjoy more stories like
Five Dares
at RiptidePublishing.com!

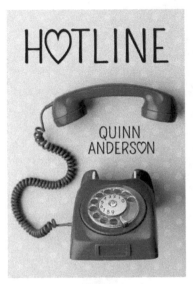
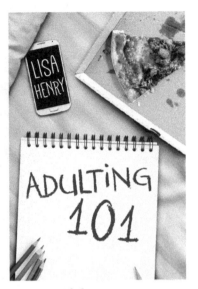